# THE
## Letter
### WITH THE
# GOLDEN
# STAMP

ONJALI Q. RAÚF

THE
Letter
WITH THE
GOLDEN
STAMP

Orion

ORION CHILDREN'S BOOKS

First published in Great Britain in 2024 by Hodder & Stoughton

7 9 10 8 6

A CIP catalogue record for this book
is available from the British Library.

ISBN 978 1 510 10892 9

Typeset in Sabon LT Std by Palimpsest Book Production Limited,
Falkirk, Stirlingshire
Printed and bound in Great Britain by
Clays Ltd, Elcograf S.p.A.

The paper and board used in this book
are made from wood from responsible sources.

Orion Children's Books
An imprint of
Hachette Children's Group
Part of Hodder & Stoughton Limited
Carmelite House
50 Victoria Embankment
London EC4Y 0DZ

An Hachette UK Company
www.hachette.co.uk

www.hachettechildrens.co.uk

For all Young Carers
Each s/heroes in a million ways.

For Abi, my former postman
And all who go far and beyond their call of duty.

And for Mam and Zak.
Always.

*The postage stamp is a flimsy thing*
*No thicker than a beetle's wing,*
*And yet it will roam the world for you*
*Exactly where you tell it to.*
– E. V. Lucas –


*. . . the greatest heroes are those who do their duty*
*. . . whilst the world whirls . . .*
– Florence Nightingale –

# CONTENTS

# 0

## The Beginning Before the Beginning

I've never been inside a real-life police station before.

I've only ever seen the one in my hometown from the outside – it's all brown and grey and empty-looking. I've seen ones on TV too. Usually on those drama programmes where everyone is always crying and screaming at each other and running away because they're in trouble. Mam calls them 'soaps', even though no one in them ever uses a single bar of soap. Not even when their faces are all runny with tears and make-up or they've been running away for days and their hands are super dirty. Just like mine are now.

The police station I'm in now is nothing like the ones I've seen on TV or the one back home. It's all shiny and clean, and so big it makes me feel like an ant trapped in a huge upside-down glass cup – except a cup that has lots of floors and lifts. There were guards at the huge front doors where I came in, standing near a giant shimmering silver sign that read 'NEW SCOTLAND YARD' – even though we aren't in Scotland and there isn't a single yard anywhere that I can see. What the sign really should have said was 'LONDON PAVEMENTS', because it's in London and has nothing but pavements all around it.

'Right then, who do we have here?'

I stare up at the police officer standing in front of me, and the large badge she has on her police cap. The badge is shining down from the middle of a black and white strip that goes all around her hat and which matches her thick, short tie. They look like chessboards that don't have any pieces on them.

'You're a long way from home, Audrey,' she continues. 'All the way from Wales, I hear?' Her eyebrows go up and disappear into her cap as if they're on board an invisible lift.

I nod at the floor instead of her, looking down at the large grey Royal Mail sack now sitting all crumpled up on my lap. I haven't let go of it since the police caught me. My fingers don't want to.

'Well, I'm Sergeant Anita,' says the officer. 'And this lady here is Ms Rogers.' Sergeant Anita points to the woman standing a little bit behind her. 'She's here to look after you while you're with us, and to make sure you have everything you need until we can get you back home.'

The lady called Ms Rogers takes a step forward. She doesn't seem like she's one of *Them* – she isn't wearing a suit or carrying a folder or looking all frowny and strict and filled with horrible questions. She's smiling, and has kind eyes and a round face, and is dressed in a woolly jumper and jeans and the kind of shiny long boots Mam used to wear before she got sick.

'Hi, Audrey. My name is Georgiana Rogers. Georgie for short. So you can call me that, all right?'

I nod again, but still can't look at either of them.

'Like Sergeant Anita said, I'm here to answer any questions you have, and help you in any way I can. So feel free to ask me anything you want to. OK?'

This time I don't even nod. Instead, I grip the sack in my hands even tighter.

3

'What you did today was incredibly dangerous,' says Sergeant Anita from above me. I see her shiny black shoes take a step towards me. 'But no one is looking to press charges or anything like that.'

'They're not?' I blurt out without meaning to, looking straight up into Sergeant Anita's face in surprise. It's long and shimmery and her large brown eyes are as shiny as her shoes.

'No,' she replies with a small smile. 'Not at all. But we do need to know *everything* that happened in the lead-up to today. What you tell us will become part of what we call a "witness statement", which will then be submitted as part of our formal proceedings.'

I stare up at Sergeant Anita, not really understanding what she's saying. What are 'formal proceedings'? And what happens when those are over? Will I still get a criminal record even if they don't press charges? Are they going to take my fingerprints? And what if some of what I have to tell them is so bad I end up in jail anyway, until I'm really old and my hair turns white?

'Now, I know you must have been very scared when we had to bring you in,' continues Sergeant Anita. 'But we've spoken to your mother, and she's sending someone to come and get you. While we're waiting—'

'But – but there isn't anyone who can come and get me,' I interrupt accidentally, quickly looking back down at the sack and my dirty hands and wishing that my silly eyes weren't burning with tears. 'My mam – she can't come . . . and I don't have anyone else. Unless . . .' Gulping hard to try and swallow down all my scariest feelings so that I can make room for some hopeful ones instead, I ask, 'Is it my tad? Is he coming to take me home? Is that who she's sent?'

'We'll have to wait and see,' says Sergeant Anita, her voice suddenly softer. 'Your mother is arranging it all, and the second the appointed person has arrived, I promise I'll notify you. But while we wait for whoever that might be, how about you tell us about the events leading up to today's incident in as much detail as you can. Exactly what happened and why. Just so we can have a nice, clear record of it all.'

'That sounds like a great idea,' says the lady called Georgie. Bending down so that her eyes can look straight into mine, she whispers, 'What do you think, Audrey? Can you tell the nice sergeant here what happened?'

I think about it for exactly six seconds. If I am going to tell my story, I'll need to start at the very beginning.

I give a slow nod.

'OK. Follow me then,' says Sergeant Anita, as she begins to walk ahead of me.

'Will – will you be with me the whole time?' I ask Georgie.

'Yes,' she replies. 'The whole time. I won't leave you until you're in a car on your way home. I promise.'

I don't really know why, but I believe her. Maybe it's because she has kind, warm eyes – a bit like Mam's – that look like they're telling the truth. Or maybe it's because I don't have any other choice. Holding on to the sack even tighter, I get up and follow Sergeant Anita.

Using a special badge that *beeps* and *boops* us through lots of doors, Sergeant Anita leads me into a room that has a table and some chairs in it. On the walls are lots of colourful pictures of police officers, smiling as if they aren't really police officers at all, but people in a toothpaste commercial. And on the table is a black box with lots of buttons on it. I want to press them all right away.

'Audrey, why don't you sit there,' says Sergeant Anita, showing me a chair. I go and sit down, wishing I could run all the way home. But then I realise I won't have anything to run back to any more. *They're* going to know everything for sure now, and take everyone I love away from me. And it's all my fault . . . The thought makes my insides feel like scrunched-up balls of paper that have been thrown into the deep end of a swimming pool.

'Right, let's start at the beginning, shall we?' suggests Sergeant Anita. Taking off her hat and placing it on the table, she opens up a long, thin notebook that's filled with scribblings and arrows and, at the centre, a great big question mark. Seeing me staring at it, she gives me a smile and flips the page over to a fresh blank sheet. 'Now, while you're talking, I'm going to take some notes. But we'll be recording this conversation too, so we can be absolutely sure that my notes don't get anything wrong. Is that all right with you?'

I look over at the Georgie lady, who gives me a nod.

I copy her and give Sergeant Anita a nod back.

'Are you ready?' asks Georgie, as she looks down at me. 'Remember, if you want to stop at any time, or you'd like a drink or to take a toilet break, all you have to do to is tell us. All right?'

I nod again.

Sergeant Anita presses a button on the black box, which makes a tiny bright-red light come on and, saying the date and time and all our names, she looks at me. 'Whenever you're ready, Audrey. Begin anywhere you want to.'

Georgie looks at me too, her eyebrows raised hopefully. Pulling my eyes away from them, I place the sack on the table, still holding it tight. As long as I hold on to it, everything will be fine.

'Anywhere?' I double-check.

'That's right,' Sergeant Anita replies. 'Anywhere at all.'

Staring at my fingers and then up at her, I open my mouth and wait for words to come out. At first, none of them do. They're stuck in a traffic jam in my throat. But then I think about Mam and how badly I need to get back to her and stop her from getting any sicker and say the most *sorry*s I've ever said in my life, and the traffic jam starts moving and beeping, and soon all the words I need are driving at top speed out of my mouth.

'Erm . . . Well . . . I – I guess it all started with the house on the other side of the street. And the spy who lives there.'

# 1

## Behind Door Number 33

'I've lived on the same street since the day I was born. It's right in the middle of Abertawe. English people call it "Swansea". Do you know it – have you been?'

Both Sergeant Anita and Georgie shake their heads in a way which makes me think that maybe they haven't been to any bit of Wales, let alone my part of it.

'Swansea is a city – but it's not like London. We don't have huge theatres or royal buildings or squares filled with lights. We've just got Plantasia and the market – oh, and the new golden bridge too. But we do have the best beaches anyone could ever want. And the hills are so steep and high that cars make a loud growling noise going up them and a happy "Weeeeeeeee!" going down them, and the houses all look like they're surfing on top of waves made of concrete. I've never lived anywhere else ever, so I know everyone on my street and what they do, which is exactly how I like it.

'Well, that is, I *used* to know everyone. But then that changed. And that's sort of what started everything, and led to me coming here and getting arrested.'

'We haven't arrested you,' corrects Sergeant Anita quickly. Her lips are doing something strange. They look like they're trying to make her nose sneeze, and her nose is fighting back. 'We just want to clarify the sequence of events that led you here, that's all. Please . . . continue. When did this change occur?'

Clutching the grey sack closer to me, I use my fingers to try and remember how many weeks ago it all started. I'm not good with dates and making days fit into weeks, so I give up and say, 'It was definitely the second day of the last school holidays. I remember because holidays are a bit boring when you can't go anywhere, so I was looking out of the window a lot. That was when I saw it for the first time. The car that magically appeared in the parking spot in front of the house – the one directly across from ours – on the other side of the street.'

I stop to watch Sergeant Anita writing something down before she looks back up at me. 'Do you mean your February half-term holiday, Audrey? Or your Christmas holidays?'

'The February one,' I reply. 'Kavi says that's a fake holiday because it's only one week and not two, and that it was teachers who invented it so they can eat all the chocolates they get on Valentine's Day in secret. Is that true?'

Sergeant Anita smiles and shakes her head, 'Not that I know of.' She pauses for a second, and then says, 'So you noticed a new car in your neighbour's driveway. Why did you think it was strange?'

'Well, I guess I didn't think it was strange right away. But after a few days I did. Because since the day it appeared, it's never been used – not even once. Why have a car if you're never going to drive it? And the curtains to the house are always drawn too, even in the daytime, and there's never even the smallest sound or bit of light coming from inside. No one has seen a single person go in or out of the bright-red front door – not even our postman.

'I know because I watched the house and the car

lots during the holidays, and when school opened again I told my two best friends at school, Inara and Kavi, all about it. I've never had anything exciting to tell them before. They argued about who the person might be a whole lot, and then decided the house had been taken over by a gang of robbers – who were going to rob the whole street until we all went blind for some reason. And that they were keeping the curtains shut to stop people from telling on them to the police and seeing all their high-tech equipment – like the walkie-talkies, and big sacks, and those spiky hooks with ropes on the end that robbers use to climb buildings.

'My little brother Peck and sister Kat – who are twins but don't look even a bit like each other – thought that the house was haunted. Peck thought it was haunted by a ghost in a white bedsheet. And Kat thought it was haunted by a group of hairy monsters who like to eat people's gardens. Whenever I picked them up from school after the day the car arrived, they always ran past the house as fast as they could – as if they were being chased. It was funny watching them do that. Especially as they're only four, and their legs are so short that when they run they look like penguins who might fall over any second.

'But I knew the people who had moved in were definitely *not* ghosts or monsters because I'm way too old to believe in silly things like that. No nine-year-old would be caught alive believing any of it. And as I told Peck and Kat, even if ghosts and monsters *did* exist, I doubt they'd have much use for a car!

'I also knew for sure it wasn't a gang of robbers like Inara and Kavi thought, because that didn't make sense either. No robber with even a half a brain would spend weeks planning to rob some boring old houses on a boring old street in Wales – not in our part of Swansea. It wouldn't be worth it. Not unless they were after some ancient TVs – or maybe those weird crystal animals that Mrs Christela at number twenty-seven collects. Plus, their car had a number plate, and if you wanted to, you could use your secret hidden CCTV spy cameras to trace it and find out who they are. Couldn't you?' I ask.

It looks like Sergeant Anita's lips are trying even harder to make her sneeze now, but she fights back again and says, 'Eh-hum. Yes . . . I'm sure we could.'

'I knew it,' I whisper, and tell my brain to remember to let Kavi and Inara know that I was right about that. 'Anyway,' I say, continuing, 'I hate not knowing things. Especially important things, like who's living across the street from me. I knew whoever was inside wasn't a ghost or a monster or a robber. *My* hypnosis told me whoever was in that house was actually . . . a spy.'

I wait for Sergeant Anita to nod at me, but instead she looks at Georgie with her eyebrows all scrunched up.

'Your . . . "hypnosis", Audrey?' asks Georgie. 'What do you mean?'

I frown back at both of them. 'You know – when your brain comes up with a way to explain things,' I say, surprised they don't know. Weren't grown-ups supposed to know all the words? 'It was my hypnosis. My guess.'

'Ah! You mean *hypothesis*,' says Sergeant Anita. As soon as she says it, I know I've said the wrong word.

'Oh! Yeah – that's what I meant.' Then, leaning to the machine, I say, 'Scratch that from the record, your honour,' just like they do on TV, and I continue.

'My hypothesis hunch told me it was an invisible

14

secret-agent spy who had moved in across the street just so they could spy on me and Peck and Kat and Mam. I didn't have any proof – not just then. It was just a feeling I got whenever I looked at the house and saw all its dark windows. You see, it's my job to know absolutely everything, because knowing everything is the only way I can keep my family – and our secret – safe.'

'Your secret?' asks Sergeant Anita, looking extra interested. Georgie is leaning in too.

I nod. It's strange being listened to by two grown-ups at the same time. Usually it's hard enough to make just one listen properly.

'I haven't got to the part where I tell you what it is yet,' I say.

'Ah! I understand,' says Sergeant Anita. 'Take all the time you need.'

'And remember, you also don't have to say anything you don't want to,' adds Georgie, her face very serious.

Remembering where I left off, I start again.

'So, our secret. I bet, because you're in the police, you have to keep lots of things secret – like about crimes and things. You probably get trained for it too.

I'm good at keeping secrets even without training. And not just that, but I have to make my little brother and sister keep our secret too. But that got harder when the spy moved in opposite, because it felt like we were being watched all the time.

'In three whole years, not a single person has found out about our secret. That's how good we are at acting like everything's OK, even on the bad days. In fact, if I was a real-life actress in Hollywood I think I'd win all the awards – even the one that *everyone* wants where you get the little statue of the man called Oscar. Because if acting is just pretending to be something you're not, then I'm definitely one of the best actresses on the planet. Plus! I don't just play one part, I play all kinds of different parts every single day. I bet the real actors and actresses don't do that.

'When I think about it for more than five minutes, I guess my mam and tad must have known that I was going to be an actress. And Peck and Kat too. It's probably why they named us after Mam's favourite movie stars, the ones who were alive hundreds of years ago and acted in old black-and-white films that were filmed before special effects were even invented. I'm named after a woman called Audrey Hepburn, and Peck is named after someone called Gregory Peck, and Kat is named after Katharine Hepburn – who, I think, might be Audrey's aunt or something, but I'm not really sure. Mam watches old movies all the time – which means I watch them all the time too. I wish I had a cool superhero name . . . like Storm. Or Raven. Or T'challa. Whoever heard of a superhero called "Audrey"? No-one, that's who.

'Anyway, a few days after the car appeared across the street, I told Mam a bit about the new neighbours and how no one ever saw them. I didn't tell her that I thought they were spies though, because I didn't want her to get worried. That's my other job, you see. As well as knowing about everything, I have to make sure Mam doesn't worry about things too much. It's not good for her. If she thinks and worries too much, her hands shake really badly and her breathing gets noisy and it scares us. So I only tell her what I absolutely have to, and the rest I try to solve myself.

'After the invisible spy moved in, I spent two whole weeks spying right back on them. Every night, after I helped Mam get dressed for bed and got all her medicines ready for the next day and checked that Peck and Kat had fallen asleep, I headed straight down to the living-room window and used the kitchen-roll tube to watch them. Have you ever used a kitchen-roll tube to spy on people? It's really hard work – especially when there's still loads of the roll left. But it didn't matter how tired I was, or how much of my homework I hadn't finished yet, or how many times my tummy growled at me because it was still hungry, I had to wait and watch and try to see who was living opposite so that we could stop worrying. But after two whole weeks of trying, I still didn't have a single clue.

'The next day, as we were leaving school, I told Inara and Kavi that I still hadn't seen anyone leave the house, and Inara said that maybe, instead of robbers, they were graveyard workers – just like her tad. She used to think her tad was like Batman because he only ever went out at night and said he was "off to fight crime!" But then she found out he worked as a security guard on a graveyard shift – which made him definitely not Batman.

'Inara is super clever but likes to pretend she's only normally clever like everyone else. She has big, round brown eyes and a mountain of curls that makes her look like a bear shaking water out of its fur whenever she shakes her head at someone. She always rubs the side of her nose whenever she thinks she's right (which is all the time). And she has a scar just above her right eyebrow – she got that from the time she rode her bike into a wall. It's been years since she found out her tad wasn't even a bit like Batman and was actually a night-time security guard, but she still hasn't got over it. So when I said my idea of the invisible neighbours being spies, she shook her curls and rubbed the side of her nose and said, "I'm telling you. They're definitely graveyard workers."

'"OR! They're robbers, like I said before, and they're staking out the street," said Kavi. He was eating a fruit pastille and chewing on it in large, round circles – just like a cow chewing grass.

'Kavi thinks any sweets that have fruit juice in them count as one of his five a day. By his count, he has at least fifty a day and is the healthiest kid in Wales. Whenever anyone wants a fruity, chewy sweet, they come to Kavi – he's famous for always having at least three packets on him. Kavi's got shiny black hair that looks like curtains, huge white teeth that pop out of his mouth whenever he smiles, and he's the shortest boy in our school. He's also the loudest.

'He said, "Did you hear about those robbers in Cardiff who took, like, fifty *million* pounds' worth of jewellery? The news people are saying they've hidden themselves with all the diamonds somewhere. What if . . . what if they're hiding right here in Abertawe – and they're staying in that house across the road from you? We're not that far away from Cardiff, you know."

'But then Inara said, "It wasn't fifty *million*! It was *fifty* pounds' worth of jewels. And they've already got caught."

'And Kavi said, "No, it wasn't! Why would a robber take just fifty pounds' worth of jewels? They're not stupid!"

'"They were stupid enough to get caught!" Inara reminded him. See, I told you she was clever.

'But Kavi wasn't convinced. "There's probably someone hiding their stash for them until they can get out of jail. I bet that's who's in there! My dad is always saying you've got to be careful when it comes to neighbours. You've got to keep your slits about you."

'"Your *what*?" asked me and Inara at the same time.

'"Your slits! These!" said Kavi, pointing to his eyes.

'"It's your *wits*," corrected Inara, rubbing the side of her nose again. "You're meant to keep your *wits* about you!"

'"Nah, that's stupid. Using your eyes is way more important than trying to be funny," argued back Kavi – even though he knew he was probably wrong. He hates being corrected by Inara, probably more than he hates salad, and he hates salad a LOT. He thinks vegetables should stay where they were found – in the ground.

'Inara was going to say something else too, but then the ice-cream van arrived. Inara loves ice cream from ice-cream vans more than anything else on the planet. If there was a fire or a zombie apocalypse or something, I'd bet you anything Inara would run straight to the nearest ice-cream van she could find and order a 99 with strawberry sauce and extra nuts before even trying to fight off any zombies or put out the fire.

'So as soon as Mrs Dimples and her ice-cream van showed up, Inara and Kavi ran off to join the crowd that had gathered all round it. Mrs Dimples isn't the real name of the ice-cream van owner – she's actually called Mrs Havens. But everyone calls her Mrs Dimples because she has the deepest dimples in Wales – it's like her face is a bowl of ice cream that someone's taken two scoops from. I always wish I could stay and have an ice cream too, but I have to pick up Peck and Kat from their class every day. And we don't have enough money for nice things like ice cream anyway.

'When I was little, I used to mind that I never got to do all the things that my friends did. But now I just focus on the important thing: getting home as quickly as possible. I'm always worrying about Mam and wondering if she's OK. There have been two times when I got home to find she wasn't, and I thought my life was over, so I always try to get home quickly.

'I waved goodbye to Kavi and Inara, picked up Peck and Kat, and we hurried home. They were telling me all about the paintings they had made in class, when suddenly Kat pulled on my arm and cried out, "Look, Old-Wee! Look!" That's what she calls me – "Old-Wee", because she's never been able to say my name right. It's the worst name anyone can *ever* be called – even by their cute baby sister, but luckily we were on our street by the time she said it that day, so there was no one from school around.

'"Look! They're moving, they're moving! The monsters are moving!"

'I stopped and looked in the direction Kat was pointing. She was pointing at the house across the street. The one with the invisible spies. Or maybe the thieves.

'I stood and stared, but couldn't see anything or anyone.

'"There's nothing there," I told Kat.

'"But it moooooooved," she wailed, as Peck nodded.

'"What moved?" I asked.

'"The kerp-tens," said Kat, pulling on my arm again. "The kerp-tens, the kerp-tens!"

'I waited and watched for a few seconds more, but there was nothing.

'"Come on," I said, not really believing her. Sometimes Kat's imagination is so strong it makes her see things like they're real when they're not. Last month she thought all the food in the lunch hall was screaming because it didn't want to get eaten. But really, it was builders on the roof using some sort of machine.

'I pulled her and Peck away, through our front garden

to the house. I wish our garden was like everyone else's on the street – all neat and clean and flowery. But except for a small bush that sprouts orange flowers whenever it feels like it, everything in our garden is pretty much dead. Even the small square patch of grass looks like straw. That means our house sticks out a lot – which isn't good when we're trying to be like everyone else. One day I'll get it fixed. Until then, the best thing about the outside of our house is our front door, which is blue. Tad painted it when I was smaller, and I still remember him letting me have a go with the brush.

'I opened it and shouted out, "Maaaaaam! We're home!" just like I always do.

'Kat ran straight upstairs, shouting "MAM! I painted in yellow!" and Peck followed her shouting out, "NO! IT WAS LOLLANGE!"

'I remember exactly what they said just then because *that* was when it happened! Peck was shouting and I was turning round to close the door when I looked out for a second. And I saw it! A pair of binoculars flashing at me from a gap in the downstairs curtain. It was only for half a second and then they disappeared – like whoever had been watching me was trying to hide.

'A second later and I would have missed it. But Kat had been right – there *was* someone there . . . and I had been right too – whoever was there was spying on us.

'I didn't know what to do so I quickly slammed the door shut and turned the key to lock it, wondering what they wanted with me and Kat and Peck and Mam! Or as everyone else on our street calls us, "the family behind door number thirty-three".'

## 2

## The Room at the Top of the Stairs

'That must have been quite frightening,' says Sergeant Anita, writing something down in her notepad. 'Did you see anything else strange that day?'

'Nope,' I say. 'I even stayed up late again so I could spy back on them, but it went back to being all silent and dark. I thought about writing about it but then I didn't.'

'Writing about it? Where?' asks Sergeant Anita.

'In my writing diary.'

Sergeant Anita looks confused, which makes me realise that she's quite old – maybe even thirty, and that maybe she had different lessons when she was a kid to the ones we have now.

'Every Monday, Mrs Li, who's my teacher, gets the

whole class to write a diary entry about all the things we got up to over the weekend. What she really means is all the *nice* things we got up to – like bowling or heading to the seaside at Mumbles or Bracelet Bay or going shopping in Cardiff. Inara and another girl in my class called Kamilah went to Disney World in America and swam with actual dolphins at Christmas, so they wrote about that in their diaries and when we all got back to school they read out pages to everyone and showed photos too. And Kavi went to Mauritius, and rode on the back of his uncle's real-life motorbike last summer – he's still writing about that, even though it was last year!

'I wish I had nice things to write in my diary, but I don't. Not really. Nice things aren't easy to do when the one person you want to do them with can't do any of it – no matter how much they might want to. So I – I make things up . . .'

I look up at Georgie, suddenly wondering if making things up in a school diary counts as a criminal offence – even if only Mrs Li reads it. But Georgie doesn't seem shocked and Sergeant Anita is nodding to encourage me to go on, so I guess it doesn't.

'I don't make up silly things,' I explain. 'It's not like I write that I have a pet unicorn or I own a castle or anything like that. I just write about normal things – like what my life could be like if we could go places and had enough money to do all the things we wanted to do. I'm not sure if Mrs Li believes everything I write in my diary – but it's fun to pretend, and on the Mondays I don't miss school, I love putting an entry in my diary. It's like I get to do all those things somehow, even if it's only in my imagination.'

'What kinds of things do you write about?' asks Sergeant Anita.

I shrug. 'Normal things. Like having a ginormous ice cream or going to the park and swinging on the swings so high that I go right over the top! Writing about those kinds of things makes everyone in my class think I'm just like them. Kavi even said that my diary was so boring it made his brain fall asleep, which is good. I want his brain – and Inara's brain and Mrs Li's brain and everyone else's too – to be so super bored by how normal I am that they all go to sleep! That way, they'll never suspect that I don't really get to do any of those things at all – not ever. And more important than any of that, they'll never ask me about Mam. It's super important they never ask me about her, because . . . well, she's my secret. *Was* my secret,' I add, realising that now everyone is going to know everything.

'And why is that, Audrey?' asks Sergeant Anita. 'Why do you try and keep your mum a secret?'

I look down at the table in front of me extra hard while my hands grip the grey sack super tight – like it's an anchor, and I can't ever let go.

'Mam . . . she's the most important person on the planet,' I say. 'At least, she is to me. But she can't leave our house much. In fact, she can't even really leave her room – the room at the top of our stairs. Not because she doesn't *want* to, but because that's where she's the safest. Mam has advanced osteoarthritis – or "Oreo-nits-us" as Peck calls it. I can say it properly because I've been saying it for years, but he's still little. That's when all the joints in your bones and all the muscles around the bones – even the tiny ones in your fingers and toes – hurt so much that it makes it super hard and super painful to move. There's no medicine that's been invented yet which can cure it, even though there's lots of doctors trying to find one, so if you have it, you can't ever get better. I know because I've learned everything I can about it from Mam and her doctor, Dr Adeola. In fact, I know so much about it that I could put on a long white doctor's coat right this minute and go to any hospital on the planet, and no one would ever know that I wasn't a doctor at all! I'd have to pretend I was a super-short doctor, but I could still do it. When I grow up I'm going to be a doctor for real and do my best to find a cure.

'Mam didn't always have her bone problem. In fact, when I was little she owned her own business and designed all kinds of things for loads of amazing companies. She even got an award one time, and in the living room there's a golden frame with a magazine cutting inside it, showing her holding up an award and shaking hands with the First Minister of Wales – who's basically like the president of the country. I love that photo of Mam, because she looks so beautiful and strong and happy that it makes *me* happy. In it, she's wearing her favourite blue trouser suit and a silky white shirt, and her hair is extra shiny, and her eyes have silver and blue glitter all the way around. That was her signature colour back then – royal blue. She used to say that if it was good enough for the royal family, it was good enough for her!

'But right after Peck and Kat were born, she started to get pains in her legs and back. And then she started not walking right, and kept on falling down, and then she was in hospital all the time and needed a cane to walk. By the time Kat and Peck were two years old and I was seven, Mam couldn't leave the house or work, so she couldn't run her business any more. And less than a year after that, she lost my tad too. Not in the park or anything. He just said he felt lost, and then Mam told him to get lost, so he left and we haven't seen him since. I figured the place he got lost in was so far away that he couldn't find a phone or even a Post Office. Except for at Christmastime, when he sends all three of us a huge box, filled right to the top with toys and books and treats. There's never a note or a message with them, but I think that's maybe because his words got lost too.

'I don't remember much about Mam before my tad left. But I do have one memory that feels like a golden sweet stored away in the cupboards of my brain. It's of me and Mam – before she got ill, being at the beach together and running really fast and her holding my hand and laughing. It's not a long memory, and sometimes I wonder if I made it up, but it feels too real to be made up. I think my brain kept it for me so I could remember the touch of Mam's hand and the sound of her laughter, because I've never been able to hold her hand properly since then. Not with my fingers going through hers anyway. And Mam never really laughs any more. She smiles a lot, but smiling's not the same thing as someone laughing so much that they sound like they're singing.

'After Tad left, it became my job to help as much as I could and keep us all together – which meant making sure no one knew about Mam's condition. Up until a few weeks ago, that didn't really mean too much work, because Mam could still do things like look after herself and walk around – even though it was hard. All I had to do was make sure she had taken all her medicines and open the bottles for her because her hands can't open the lids any more. And sometimes cook dinner. I tried to roast a chicken once, but it set itself on fire, so after that I stuck to things that came in a packet and are easy to cook. Luckily Mam's favourite meals are fish finger sandwiches or chicken-flavoured noodles from a packet, and I can make those easy. She used to be able to do everything else by herself, but now she needs more help, like with cutting up her food, or carrying her cup of tea or walking upstairs – because sometimes her hands start shaking and she spills things or she falls down.

'Some days we used to have what Mam calls a Sunshine Day. That's when her bones feel like there's a strong bit of sun heating them all up and she's not in too much pain, and I can go to school without worrying. And when we get home, Mam's usually downstairs and she cooks us tea. Mam's always telling us how much she loves us, but on Sunshine Days she tells us that *and* she gives us a *cwtch* too – that's an extra-special cuddle that you can only get in Wales.

'But most days aren't Sunshine Days, especially now. They're Annoying Days, which means Mam can't move that much and feels annoyed at herself. On those days, as soon as I get back from school I try to do everything and stay with her all the time. Peck and Kat stay too, but sometimes they get bored, so they go off and play games on their own. They're pretty good at doing things without needing me all the time now, which makes it lots easier. When they were smaller, it was hard keeping them off Mam and away from her hurting bones.

'The worst days are the Nightmare Days. That's when Mam is in so much pain everything feels like a nightmare to her – and to us too. On those days Mam says even breathing is painful, and she has to squeeze her eyes tight and sometimes even scream to let the pain out of her. One time I asked her what it felt like, and she said it's like a horrible creature with hot, sharp claws is twisting and wringing every single one of her bones tighter and tighter and tighter – even the small bones in her face – and they don't stop, not even when she feels as if she might break. And all she can think about for as long as the pains last is how to survive through to the next second and the next minute. When that happens, and the monsters inside her are twisting her all up and hurting her so much, sometimes even her medicines don't help. I'd do anything to make those claws let go of her. It's the worst thing – not being able to do anything. All I can do is make sure that Kat and Peck are extra quiet and stay away from her on Nightmare Days, because it's not nice to see her like that. Even I find it scary, which means they must find it even scarier.

'Ever since Mam told me about what a Nightmare

Day feels like, I never go to school on those days. And I don't go in on the days Mam lies to me either. See, sometimes she tries to pretend she's not in pain so I don't miss any more lessons. But lucky for me, she's not as good an actress as I am. I always try to at least get Kat and Peck to school, but some days everything's so horrible I can't think straight, so they have to miss everything too. They don't usually mind – except if there's an assembly they were meant to be in, or birthday cupcakes they have to miss. But we all get over it when we see Mam hurting so badly . . .

'Wait! You can't put me in jail for missing school, can you? And you can't punish Mam just because she needs me to look after her sometimes! Can you?' I ask, suddenly feeling frightened that I've said too much.

Sergeant Anita shakes her head, her eyes looking extra shiny.

'No, Audrey. No one would punish you for wanting to look after your mother when she's so ill. It's always for schools to decide how to deal with such a situation, and most will try to help. So don't worry about that at all.'

Feeling relieved, I let go of the grey sack slightly. My

hands have begun to turn red and sore from holding on to it so tightly.

'Well, we do get help – from Dr Adeola. He comes to see Mam once a week to make sure everything's OK and check on her medicines. Mam always tries to act extra strong in front of him, and I know it's because she doesn't want *Them* to take us away from her. So whenever Dr Adeola comes, I make the house extra neat and tidy too.'

'Who do you mean by *Them*, Audrey?' asks Georgie, gently putting a hand on my arm.

'The social officers. You know, the ones that spy on you and try to catch you doing things wrong so they can take you away from your family,' I reply, surprised. Surely everyone who works in a police station knows about *Them*?

'And why do you think the social services would send spies to watch you?' asks Sergeant Anita.

'I've seen it,' I say. 'On the telly in a programme that Mam watched one time. There were these people from the social teams, and they were doing stakeouts with big binoculars and telescopes – and hiding behind curtains just like the person behind the red door across the street from us was doing.' I lean forward and make my eyes go big at Sergeant Anita. 'They were trying to catch this family who were stealing money benefits and cheating people. And then when they did catch them, they split the whole family up and the mam and tad had to go to jail. I think whoever's inside the house across the road from us thinks we might be doing that – but we're not. Mam would never ever do anything wrong. She's not a criminal.'

I fall quiet. If I was braver, I would say that Mam isn't a criminal but *I* am. I'm the one *They* might be trying to catch because of everything I've done. And that if anyone is going to be the reason for my family getting split up, it's going to be me. But the words won't come out. I'm not brave enough yet.

Sergeant Anita underlines something in her notebook and then looks at me. 'Does anyone else except Dr Adeola know of your mum's condition?'

I shake my head.

'Not even your school?' asks Georgie.

I shake my head again. 'Mrs Li knows that Mam can't come to the school to drop us off or come to parents' evenings and things, and Mr Garcia – that's our head teacher – knows that too. But I told them it's because Mam is busy with work. That's the other thing I write in my school diary – that Mam has a really important job. Only Dr Adeola knows the truth – and he'd never tell on us. I checked once, and he said he took a hypocritical oath, which means he can't ever tell other people about any of us. Not unless our lives are in danger. He's the only other person who knows about Mam's Nightmare Days, and that when those happen I have to become a nurse, and a cook, and a cleaner, and a shopper, and a bath-giver, and a bins-putter-outer, and a medicine-picker-upper, and a cash-from-a-cash-machine-getter, and a story-time teller, and a babysitter, and a tea-maker, and a bills payer . . .'

*And sometimes a criminal too – but only when I absolutely have to*, I say to myself.

'But my main-*main* job is to be a bodyguard and to protect the house and Mam and Peck and Kat. I can't ever let anyone take Mam away from us. Not ever. That's why I came here – to London. And that's why I need to find out who is in the house across the road and why they're hiding and using binoculars and flashing lights and things.'

'Flashing lights?' asks Sergeant Anita, leaning forward.

I nod. 'I've seen them twice now. Strange, bright white lights flashing in the upstairs window – in the room exactly opposite to Mam's. The last time was two nights ago . . . and the first time was a few days after Kavi and Inara had the argument about the Cardiff jewellery robbers. I was on my graveyard shift like normal, and then I saw them – three flashes before everything went dark. I didn't tell anyone. It scared me too much. I watched all the rest of that week but didn't see anything else, and by Sunday, I was too tired to stay up all night so I went and sat with Mam instead. That was the night I got my first big idea.

'I've told you that Mam loves watching the same movies again and again, haven't I?'

Sergeant Anita and Georgie both nod.

'But I haven't told you just how many *times* she's watched them! I would say she's watched all of her favourite films at least three hundred times. Which means I've watched them three hundred times too. When she puts one I've already seen on, my brain kind of switches off, and I only act like I'm watching, when really I'm thinking about lots of other things. That night – a few days after the flashing lights – when I went and sat with her, she said, "Let's watch a classic tonight. How about something of yours?"

'By that she meant a film with the real Audrey in it. So I picked my favourite one. Have you ever seen *Charade*?'

Sergeant Anita frowns and Georgie shakes her head.

'Oh, that's the best movie! It's got the most clever ending ever. I've watched it so many times and I still love it. After I put it on, I sat next to Mam and gave her a gentle cwtch that wouldn't hurt her, and we began watching it.

'But I must have been tired because my eyes began to close and the inside of my head got all fuzzy and dark. I would have fallen asleep if Mam hadn't suddenly laughed and said, "Ha! Right in front of his nose and he can't smell it."

'When she said that, I woke up and saw one of the spies on the telly shaking the real Audrey's handbag, and an envelope falling out of it.

'*That* was when it happened – the idea that started everything. It was as if my brain was being shaken too and I suddenly realised that doing graveyard shifts to find out about the spy across the street was silly. What I should have been doing was being like Audrey in the film and looking for clues in *everything* – especially people. You see, in the movie, nearly everyone's a walking piece of evidence, and the real Audrey has to put all the pieces together to find the truth. And the more I thought about it, the more I realised that I already knew lots of people on my street, and there was bound to be someone who knew something about the spy across the street – even if they didn't *know* they did.

'And in a flash I knew *exactly* who that someone was. It was so obvious I didn't know why my brain hadn't thought of it sooner! All I had to do was wait until morning, and put on some extra-large sunglasses. And if I got my acting just right, I would know who the curtain-twitching ghost was in no time, and why they were spying and flashing lights at the one room it was my job to protect, no matter what.'

# 3

## The Postman Who Always Knocks Twice

'Do *you* have a postman?' I ask, looking up at Sergeant Anita. 'Are they nice?'

Sergeant Anita looks over at me and smiles. 'Well, I'm not sure. I've never really met my postman – or postwoman.'

'Really? Never ever, EVER?' I ask, feeling shocked and sorry for her.

'I work quite long hours,' she explains. 'So I'm never at home when they call.'

'Is that the same for you too?' I ask Georgie.

Georgie taps her chin before answering, making the great big purple stone on her ring shine out at me.

'No – I've met all my postmen and postwomen,' she says. 'But in my area they keep changing – just when

I've got to know one, a new one hops along. They've always been lovely though.'

'I'm glad,' I say. 'I think they're some of the most special people ever. I know that because of *my* postman. Every single morning from Monday to Saturday, at exactly eight fifteen a.m., he knocks on the door. He has to knock because the bell's broken and I don't know how to fix it. I can tell it's him and not someone else, because he's always exactly on time, and he always knocks once, then waits exactly two seconds before knocking again. His knock is so loud it makes the house shiver as if it's just climbed into a freezing cold bath.

'I also know it's him because no one else ever knocks on our door. Except for Mrs Christela who lives three doors down, and that's only at Christmastime to drop off a card. Mrs Christela's knock goes *tappety-tap-tap*, as if she's tapping out a secret code, and it's so soft she always has to do it at least three or four times before we hear her. I like how people's knocks are all different, like fingerprints. Mine is two loud ones before I go quiet and wait, and Inara's is one giant one. Kavi goes on knocking right up until the door's opened and

43

sometimes even afterwards. I guess you could copy other people's knocks, but I bet it'd still sound different. Maybe it's the hand doing the knocking that makes each one sound like the person it belongs to. If I wasn't going to be a doctor, I'd be a scientist and try and find out all about it.

'My postman's name is Mo – he's been our postman ever since I can remember, and every day when I open the door to him he always says, "Good morning, little madam! It's Mo here!", as if it's the first time we're meeting each other and not the three millionth time.

'I think Mo is one of my most favourite grown-ups ever – second only to Mam. He's always smiling and he has the biggest smile I've ever seen. It's so big it's like he's trying to show everyone all his shiny white teeth at once. And he has the crinkliest eyes, which have bags under them shaped like cashew nuts. He smiles even when it's raining and snowing, or when he's so hot he looks like he's melting. The only time he's not smiling is when he's just run away from Mrs Lumley's dog. Mrs Lumley lives opposite and a few doors down, and her dog thinks it's fun to chase everyone. I especially like way Mo tips his cap to me when he says goodbye – as if I'm someone important and special, even though I'm not.

'But the best ever thing I like about Mo is that once or twice a week he gives me a brand-new stamp to add to my collection.

'I love stamps, I do. Even more than chocolate, or the fizzy sweets my friends bring to school for me to try. Even if I had a million sweets, it wouldn't beat the way I feel when I see a new stamp. Especially when it's winking at me from the corner of an envelope. I'm not sure if there's a word for that kind of feeling – I don't think it's been invented yet. For when your insides feel like the roar of an entire football stadium of people seeing the winning goal to the World Cup being scored. That's exactly how I feel whenever I see a brand-new stamp.

'I can't remember how old I was when I first began collecting stamps. All I know is, by my seventh birthday I had a whole envelope full of them. Before Mam started to get ill, she would ask all her friends to save me any that looked different and interesting – especially from any countries outside Wales. When my grandparents were alive they lived on the other side of the planet in

New Zealand, so every year for Christmas and my birthday I was sure to get a stamp that had travelled all the way from there to our doorstep. That was like magic, that was. To think that it had travelled more miles than anyone I knew! And no stamp that came from them was ever the same. Not ever. Which is what I love about stamps the most: they're always changing, with new designs and pictures and colours being invented – even different shapes – as if each stamp is a new scene from a movie, telling a story that won't ever end. And the more different each stamp is from all the other stamps, the better it is for my collection.

'The envelope of stamps I had when I was seven is now a whole shoebox thanks to Mo, and he's the only one who knows about it too. Until yesterday, not even Mam or Kavi or Inara knew about my collection, and I always kept it hidden from Kat and Peck in case they found it and ruined all the stamps by accident.

'I don't know why I didn't want anyone except Mo to know, but I guess it's because I'm worried other people will laugh at me or think that I'm not cool. After all, whoever heard of a cool stamp collector? No one, that's who. I'm not even sure if Mo thinks it's cool, but I think he does, because sometimes he winks and says, "Better keep that one safe, Audrey! None of the other collectors would ever let go of that one!" And he always looks excited when he finds one that we both know I haven't got yet. Thanks to him, I've got over two hundred stamps from around the world to look at – which is kind of like having my very own art gallery. Except one that's small enough to fit in a shoebox.

'I never know on what days Mo will have a stamp for me, so whenever I hear his knock, it feels as though something special might happen. Usually when he knocks, I'm busy helping Kat and Peck get their school bags ready or checking on Mam's medicines and I have to rush to get to the door. But on the morning after having my brilliant *Charade* idea, I woke up extra early to get all my chores done, and I even found Mam's sunglasses to wear. The other Audrey – the real one – wears extra-big sunglasses in lots of her movies to help her look mysterious and cool, so I wanted to do it too.

'I was so ready that morning that I opened the door before Mo even had a chance to do his second knock.

Mo said his usual "Well, good morning, little madam! It's Mo here! Got just these for you today."

'I looked up through Mam's giant sunglasses as he pulled out a small thin envelope and a flyer for half-price pizza. Most days, all we ever get are leaflets and adverts. I did tell Mo we don't need them and that they all go in the recycling bin anyway, but he still keeps bringing them over. And he always knocks on the door instead of just pushing them through the letterbox too.

'"Thank you," I said, as I took them from him and waited for him to ask me the same question he always asks me every single day.

'"Everyone here all right then? A little too sunny for you this morning, is it?" he added, frowning and looking over his shoulder at the dull grey sky behind him.

'"I'm being fashionable," I explained.

'And Mo said, "Ah!" and nodded seriously. "I'll take your word for it, little miss – and hers too." The "her" he meant was Kat, because she had come racing down the stairs, and on seeing Mo had run into him at full speed.

'"Hello, other little madam," said Mo. "You all right?"

'Kat nodded and replied. "I'm having peanut butter sandwiches today. Old-Wee made them!"

'"That's nice," said Mo, pretending not to hear how she said my name. He always pretended not to hear when she said my name wrong. That's another thing I like about him. "Peanut butter is good for you – it will help you build up those strong bones of yours."

'Kat jumped up all happy and asked, "Like fwamingos and lions?"

'"Exactly," said Mo, letting his smile take over his whole face again.

'"I'm going to eat more then," cried out Kat, before running away back upstairs to tell Mam and Peck. When she was gone, Mo gave a chuckle and then went back to being all serious. He told me he didn't have any stamps for me that day, but that Mrs Nayar on the street over was expecting a package from her daughter in Brazil soon, and that she'd already agreed to let him have the stamps, so he'd have a new one for me soon.

'I'd never had any stamps from Brazil before, so I was well excited and said, "Thank you, Mo!"

'As he reached up to tip his cap at me, Mo's eyes wandered all over the house behind me. They always did that just before he was about to leave – as if they were security cameras making sure that nothing was missing.

'"Wait, before you go!" I exploded. "Can I – ask you something?"

'I stood up extra straight like the other Audrey always does and tried not to look even a little bit nervous. It's hard to look normal and calm when you feel like there's a thousand worms all squiggling and wriggling inside you, isn't it? I was glad I was wearing sunglasses – it meant Mo could only see half of my face, so I didn't need to worry about him looking into my eyes and seeing the truth.

'"You can ask me anything you like, little miss," Mo said, dropping his hand before it touched his cap.

'"I . . . I was wondering . . . do you know who lives in the house on the other side of the street?"

'Mo turned round to look, asking me, "Which one do you mean?"

'"The one with the red door – number forty-two," I said, pointing straight at it.

'"Oh?" Mo's eyebrows dived into a frown – like they were confused by my question.

'"Yeah. I – I was wondering if you knew who they were – like what their name is and what they do and things . . ."

'Mo said, "Ah, you were *wondering*, were you? Why's that then?"

'Then I lied – but I hadn't meant to! It was one of those lies that slip out of your mouth before your brain has even thought of it. "I wanted to say hello to them because they're new and everything," said my mouth – not me. "And welcome them to the neighbourhood?"

'I got nervous then, and gripped the envelope and pizza advert super tight, hoping that the question at the end didn't sound like a question at all.

'But I didn't need to worry. Mo believed me right away. "Well now, that's nice of you," he said. "But there's not much I can tell you, I'm afraid. I haven't met them yet."

'"You haven't?" I was well disappointed. I thought if anyone would have seen them, it would be Mo. "Do you know their names then – like from their envelopes?" I tried. I was sure he did. There's no way you can post an envelope or a postcard through someone's door without reading the name and address.

'Mo looked at me with one eyebrow slowly rising up across his forehead.

'I tried to act like the question was no big deal. If I had been the real Audrey in a film, I would have walked off looking all cool and smart – to show him how much I really didn't care. But I couldn't do that, so I pushed Mam's sunglasses up further near my eyeballs instead. I've seen people do that in movies too.

'"Well, as it happens, I do know their name," Mo replied. "I couldn't deliver their letters without knowing, now, could I? But it's confidential information, see? I'm afraid I'd be breaking the law if I told you."

'"What? There's a law about telling me a *name*? Really?" I asked.

'Mo laughed and nodded. He said that post people have lots of laws that they have to follow – some of them going back hundreds of years! Kind of like the police, I guess – maybe that's why you both have to wear uniforms?'

Sergeant Anita smiles. 'Maybe. It's true that we both have many laws we have to follow. Your postman Mo was right to not tell you the name, Audrey.'

I nod. 'I know. Mo told me. He said, "Nobody can

break the rules of the Royal Mail or the Post Office, little miss. Especially not those of us who get to work for them."

'That made me surprised and disappointed at the same time, but then Mo stuck his cap back on his head, and whispered, "But there's nothing stopping you from going over and knocking on the door yourself now . . . or posting a message of your own, is there? I'll even deliver it for you if you like and make it official."

'When I got to school that day, I told Kavi and Inara all about what Mo had said. Inara thought knocking on the door and just asking was a brilliant idea, but Kavi didn't like it one bit. He shook his head and tried to warn me by saying, "There could be robbers and murderers inside, remember?" Then he asked me did I never watch a programme called *Crimewatch* and was I crazy, and said, "It's super dangerous, it is, to go knocking on strangers' doors. Especially at night. There might be a crazy cereal-chomping killer there, and what if they use a walking stick to hit you and then say it was too dark and they never saw you?"

'I told him I wasn't that *twp* – that means daft in Welsh, you know – and that I'd never go knock on a door at night-time. And Inara argued back too and said, "It's not like she's going to a house in the middle of a field – it's only across the street. Besides, Wales doesn't have any cereal-killers. They all live in England."

'But I thought Kavi was half right. Even if I wasn't going at night, I needed to be careful, because none of us knew who was living in there. So I interrupted their arguing to ask if they could both come with me after school that day to go knock on the door together.

'Inara was surprised and asked, "Really? You're going to let us walk home with you for the first time ever?"

'I'd forgotten that I'd never let her or Kavi know what street I lived on, let alone walk there with me. So I said, "Yeah. But we're only going to knock on the door. You can't come to my house. Mam's too busy to have anyone over – you know, with work." They nodded, which made me super relieved. When I'm older and have some money, I'll make everything nice and fill Mam's house with cool things. Then I can have friends over and maybe even have a sleepover. It's always been my dream to have a sleepover. But I couldn't let them come in yet.

'After they both said they'd come with me, Kavi

puffed his chest out like a chicken who was about to lay an egg. He said he was coming to protect us – which made me and Inara laugh. Don't tell him I told you – especially not since you're the police, but Kavi screamed at his own shadow in the Halloween assembly last year. If anyone needed protecting, it was going to be him – and probably from himself too. We would have gone on laughing, I think, but then Nutan – who's in the class next door and is super fast and is always playing something – came over to us and said, "Hey, Audrey, Inara, Kavi! Want to play foot-base with us?"

'We all nodded because we love foot-base.'

'Sorry, Audrey, what's foot-base?' asks Sergeant Anita, looking up from her notepad.

'Oh. I forget you're old . . . er! OLDER!' I add, feeling my face go red. Sergeant Anita and Georgie both grin and I can tell they know what I had tried to cover up.

'Erm . . . it's like baseball mixed with football. You run around bases to try and get a home run – but instead of hitting a ball with a bat you kick a football,' I explain quickly. 'Nutan says she invented it, but Nutan says she also invented bubblegum when she was a baby after she blew bubbles out of her own drool, so no one really believes her.'

'Ah,' says Sergeant Anita.

'It was good Nutan asked us to play, because I had so much energy that I could have kicked at least twenty footballs and run to fifty bases. And while I waited my turn and watched everyone kicking and shouting and trying to get to last base, I started to think about who might be waiting for us behind the red door. Would it be a jewel-thief who didn't really know or care anything about me or Mam? Or just a super-nosy, super-quiet neighbour? Or would it really be one of *Them*, waiting to catch me out for all the things I'd done and take me away from Mam? My insides told me it had to be *Them*. Even a thief or a super-secret neighbour would still need to leave the house sometimes or use their car to go and get things. Trained spies wouldn't. They wouldn't need to go anywhere . . .

'When Nutan shouted out that it was my turn, I walked up to home base – which was just Jacob's rucksack – and waited. She threw her big purple football at me with an extra-hard and extra-twangy bounce.

'I kicked it as hard as I could and ran so fast that

my legs felt like they were a blur. I love it when my legs feel like that. I bet it's how birds feel right before they start flying. I stopped at the third rucksack-base, just in time to not get caught, and watched Larry getting ready for his turn. But I wasn't really watching him at all. I was just acting as if I was. Because in my mind I didn't see the playground, or the players, or the purple football. I was too busy imagining the red door that was waiting for me and Kavi and Inara to knock our own special knocks on it, and all the different faces of the person who might be hiding behind it.'

# 4

## A Message in a Ninja Bottle

'And did you go and knock on it that day?' asks Sergeant Anita, looking super interested.

I nod. 'We knocked and knocked and knocked! And we rang the doorbell too, but no one opened the door. Kavi even stood on his tiptoes and pressed his face right up against the windows, but he couldn't see a thing. Only his own face. He kept saying, "Maybe they're sleeping. We should go! Mam's always saying you should let sleeping butchers lie."'

'Sleeping butchers?'

I shrug my shoulders at Sergeant Anita's question. 'Me and Inara don't bother asking Kavi where he gets all his sentences from.'

Sergeant Anita smiles and writes something else down. 'Please go on.'

'Well . . . Inara had been counting how many times we knocked on the door and rang the doorbell. She said it was seventeen times ringing and forty-three times knocking, and that we should stop or we might break the bell. So we stopped and looked up at the windows for any sign that our super-knocking had worked. But everything was still and silent like always – as if the house itself had got the hump with us and crossed its arms.'

'Where were Kat and Peck?' asks Georgie.

'They were there with us. Kat was pulling on Inara's arm because she wanted to get lifted up to ring the doorbell again, and Peck was clinging on to Kavi's back and pretending Kavi was a camel. They were both acting super naughty, but I think they were excited because Inara and Kavi were on our road. I was going to ring the doorbell just one more time when someone shouted, "Oi! What you kids up to there?"

'That made us all jump, that did! It was Mr Llewelyn who lived three doors down – he was at the garden gate and staring at us like he was proper angry. Mr

Llewelyn is famous on my street for two things: hiding his extra rubbish bags in everyone else's bins, and being able to squeeze his huge white builders' van into the tiniest parking spots. Mam says he's lived on our street forever and has fixed half the houses in Wales. He definitely looks it, because his face is like the trunk of an old tree that lots of people have scratched their initials into, his fingernails are always dirty and powdery, and he never ever wears anything except dark blue dungarees with a million paint marks on them.

'Inara was the quickest one to answer back. She said, "We just wanted to say hello to the new neighbours."

'And I added, "I'm from over there," and pointed across the street to my blue door, in case he didn't remember who I was. I could see Kavi and Inara looking over at my door as well – which made me realise it was the first time they were seeing it too.

'"I know where you three are from. But what about these two?" asked Mr Llewelyn, pointing at Kavi and Inara.

'"They're my friends," I explained.

'"BEST friends," added Inara.

'Mr Llewelyn nodded and opened his mouth, but

before he could say another word I realised he could be my next piece of walking evidence. After all, Mr Llewelyn only lived three doors down from number forty-two, which meant his back garden was only three gardens over. And *that* meant he could definitely see everything. All the gardens on my street are tiny and long and sloping because of the hill we're on, and the walls are so low that everyone can see each other's gardens for at least ten houses down.

'So I asked, "Have YOU seen the people living here, Mr Llewelyn? Like – maybe in the *garden*?" I made my eyes go bigger when I asked that second question for extra effect, because the detectives on telly always make their eyes go either smaller or bigger when they're asking important questions.

'Mr Llewelyn shook his head. "Not seen hide nor cap of them. Don't think they've been out back at all. But that doesn't surprise me. Most people like to keep themselves to themselves. So come away now – and give them some peace. And, er . . . you might want to stop her from doing that," he added, nodding past my shoulder.

'It was Kat. She was pushing handfuls of grass

through the letterbox and whispering, "Hello, monsters! Eat these!"

'I ran over and, pulling her away, hurried out of the gate with Kavi and Inara.

'"Good," said Mr Llewelyn. "Better safe than in trouble!" Giving a nod, he walked off towards his house.

'"Well, that was useless," said Inara.

'"Yup," agreed Kavi.

'But I didn't think so. After all, we had found out one piece of evidence – which was that whoever was in the house never used the garden. That made them even more suspicious. Everyone knew that Mr Parks, who had lived there before, had put actual real bamboo in his garden – and a small water fountain he had brought all the way from Japan. Nobody else in the whole of Swansea probably had anything like that in their garden! So why would someone living there not want to use it? I was going to tell Inara and Kavi all this, when Kavi asked, "What do we do now?"

'I shrugged, looking around for another neighbour to get more evidence from. But the street was empty except for us.

'Kat started pulling on my arm just then – I think

she wanted to go home. I shouted, "Be quiet, Kat! I'm trying to think!" which was totally the wrong thing to say, because as soon as I said it Kat's face turned into an extra-ripe strawberry and her mouth turned itself into a trumpet and she started blasting out lots of cries.

'I was afraid Mam would hear her from the bedroom window, so I begged her to shush and promised her a chocolate bar for tea. Peck started crying because he wanted one too, so I said, "You'll BOTH get one – as long as you stop crying *right now*!"

'That worked instantly – Kat stuck her whole hand in her mouth and Peck clasped his hands over his mouth too. It's not every day that I give them chocolate, see – only on extra-special days.

'Inara looked well impressed with me and said, "Bribery. Nice!"

'"It's the only way sometimes," I said, thinking about what to do. I remembered what Mo had suggested. "I know. Let's leave them a message."

'Kavi and Inara agreed that was the only good idea left, so Inara opened her backpack and pulled out her favourite bright-yellow giraffe pen, and I ripped out a page from my homework diary.

'"What shall I write?" I asked.

'"Maybe invite them to dinner?" said Kavi. "Wait! No – if they see inside your house they might want to steal everything. So don't do that."

'"And DON'T tell them you've been watching them," said Inara. "Or that we think they might be robbers."

'"Or that Kat's been pushing grass through the door," said Kavi.

'"Great! Now I've got pages of all the things I *shouldn't* write! How about all the things I *should*?" I asked.

'"Maybe ask them something they need to answer," suggested Inara. "That way when they answer back, we can get more information about them."

'We all looked back up at the house, wondering what question we could ask that would make someone answer back *and* not make us look suspicious. And I had to make sure we asked a question so clever and so normal that it would confuse *Them* into thinking me and Mam and Kat and Peck were a normal family. The problem was, I couldn't think of anything. I could see Inara and Kavi were stuck too, because they both kept opening and closing their mouths like fish with nothing to say.

'But then Kat helped – without even meaning to. Because that was when I caught her licking the car parked behind us it like it was a giant, dusty lollipop. I pulled her back right away and told her off, but she kept shouting, "It's yummy!" and then tried to lick Inara too.

'"No more licking things, OK?" I told her. "Especially not that – it's disgusting and dirty!" The car was covered in so much dust its bright-blue colour had faded to a brown-grey. It almost looked as depressed and as sad as the house it belonged to.

'And then suddenly my brain began to fizz and pop and jump like popcorn in a giant hot saucepan. Grabbing Inara's pen and the diary page, I wrote:

Dear neighbur,
    Would you like your car washed for free? It's super derty. My friends would like to help too.
    From Audrey (in the house with the blue door across the street.) Please write back at your earlyest conveyneyance.

'When Inara saw what I'd written she said, "Wicked! Grown-ups love getting stuff for free."

'"Yeah," said Kavi. "Mam's always trying to make me wash her car and hoover it too, but I told her child slavery's against the law."

'I folded the note in half. "I wish we had an envelope to put it in so that it would look all proper and professional and serious," I said.

'"We can make one out of another bit of paper?" suggested Inara. She was opening her bag to see what she had, when Kavi shouted out, "Wait! I've got a better idea!" He made Peck let go of his ears and slide back down off his back, and then took out his favourite Teenage Mutant Ninja Turtles water bottle from his rucksack. Pouring out the tiny bit of water that was inside, he gave it a polish with his sleeve so that the turtles posing all along the outside of the clear bottle glistened and shone and smiled even harder in their different ninja poses.

'"Go on," he said. "You can put your message in this."

'"In your water bottle?" I asked, confused. "But why?"

'He rolled his eyes. "If there are loads of letters on the floor already, this'll make ours stand out. When we got back from Mauritius, Dad had to push our door extra hard because we had so many letters, and he took forever opening them because they all looked so boring. This will make our one look like maybe a pirate's sent it to them from their ship. It'll be way too interesting not to open right away."

'Inara was so surprised by how clever it all was her eyebrows nearly jumped off her face! Saying "Good one, Kavi," she gave him a punch on the arm, snatched the note from my hands, rolled it up and put it inside the bottle.

'"This is gonna be the coolest message anyone will ever get!" said Kavi. He looked excited, but I could tell he was also just realising he had given his favourite bottle away.

'"Thanks, Kavi – it *is* going to be the coolest ever! I bet *no one's* put a message in a bottle like this one before!" I said. That made him smile a bit more.

'"You do it," ordered Inara, rubbing the side of her nose and pushing the bottle into my hands. "Go on. They're your weirdo neighbour."

'I nodded and, with everyone staring at me like they were a family of giant garden gnomes, I ran back up to the red door and pushed the bright-green faces of the ninja turtles through the golden letterbox. I waited for a second to hear it land safely on the other side and was just about to run back when I heard something else . . . it was like a loud whizzing, buzzing sound – heading straight towards me from inside the house!

'I put my ear to the door. The buzzing grew louder and louder – it sounded like an angry wasp that was about to crash right through the wood. Suddenly there was a thud – like something had banged into the door! I was too scared to stay a second longer, so I screamed and ran off, making everyone scream and run down the road right after me.'

## 5

## The Welsh Inquisition

'Can you describe the buzzing noise for me a bit more, Audrey?' asks Sergeant Anita.

I close my eyes and try to remember the sound. 'It was just like a . . . *BZZZZZZ-BZZZZZZZZZZZZ* noise. Quiet at first, and then louder and louder.'

Sergeant Anita's forehead crinkles up like a hair scrunchie. 'Did it sound machine-like at all?'

I nod. 'After I explained to everyone what I heard and why I had run away, Kavi said it might have been one of those robots the army use to blow up suspicious packages. He was well excited at first, but then he realised his bottle might get blown up. And Inara said it might have been a drone because drones sound like wasps and maybe the drone was coming to pick the post up. Or a robot hoover – but like a big one that could hoover up a whole bottle. And then Kavi changed his mind and said that he thought it was a drill – and that the robbers were drilling tunnels from number forty-two to everyone else's houses.'

'That's a lot of theories for you all to think up,' says Georgie, looking impressed.

'Yeah. I remember them all because I wrote them all down in my evidence book. It's kind of like yours,' I say, pointing at Sergeant Anita's notebook. 'Except mine has small red dragons all over it – and elephant stickers Inara gave me because elephants are my favourite animal. They never forget things – not like people. My tad got the notebook for me for Christmas last year and I was saving it for something special. I wrote down all our theories in it, and all my questions for the inquisition I did – and what everyone said right back. I did bring it with me to London, but I think it fell out of the box – you know, when I ran away from everyone? If I still had it, I could remember things better.'

'You're doing a fantastic job even without it,' says Sergeant Anita, writing something down and drawing a big circle around it. 'But tell me, what do you mean when you say you "did an inquisition"? Who else did you make inquiries of?'

'Oh. Well, after the weird buzzing sound and talking to Mr Llewelyn, my suspicions got really high – like a thermometer when you have a fever. So the next morning, when Mo knocked on our door at the usual time, I had a whole new plan. I asked him about the people who lived *near* the house with the red door instead. I figured that even if Mo didn't know anything about who was at house number forty-two, one of the neighbours might. I think neighbours stop being neighbours when they live more than three doors away, so I just asked about the doors numbered . . .' I scrunch my eyes tight to remember the numbers correctly. 'Thirty-six to forty on the left side of the house, and forty-four to forty-eight on the other side. And actually, I'd already talked to Mr Llewelyn at number forty-eight and I knew Mrs Lumley was at number forty-four, so it was really just one house on the right side I needed to know about – number forty-six – and then three houses on the left side.

'Mo looked all suspicious again and wanted to know why I was asking, so I told him it was for school. I think he guessed I was still trying to find out about whoever was behind the red door, but he didn't seem to mind. He just said that everyone on the street was really nice, but that I was to be careful at number forty because they had a cat that liked to hiss at people, though if I didn't look at it in the eyes and walked past it really slowly, I would be fine. And that at number forty-six there was a new baby, so I shouldn't be shocked at how the people living there looked because they hadn't slept in three months.

'I put everything Mo said in my notebook right away, but I wanted to see if *They* would send a message back first before I did anything else. Inara said that was a good idea, so we waited, and waited, and waited some more. All that week, Kavi kept asking about his bottle, but I didn't get anything back from across the road. Not on Tuesday, or Wednesday or on Thursday. By Friday, Inara said waiting had been a stupid idea and I needed to make a new plan fast before the memento was gone. So when Saturday morning came and Mo had been – and given me a stamp all the way from Turkey! – and there was *still* no message in a bottle back, I decided I couldn't wait any more.

'After breakfast I grabbed my evidence book and told Mam I had to interview some neighbours for a homework project and that I'd only be a short while. She said that was fine, because Mam knew most of the neighbours from before she fell ill, even though she didn't let them in the house any more. I was just ready to leave when Kat and Peck starting moaning that they wanted to come too. Little brothers and sisters can be well annoying. I didn't want to take them because I wouldn't look like a professional undercover detective any more, but I knew I had to or they'd never leave Mam alone. Whoever's heard of a detective that has to babysit at the same time they're detecting? No one, that's who. I bet no police detective person here has ever had to do it. But Mam made them promise to be on their best behaviour, so I said they could come. I took Mam's big sunglasses again – I figured they made good investigation glasses and put them on. Then, grabbing my favourite pencil and Kat and Peck, I headed to the first house on the left hand-side I wanted to interview: number thirty-six.

'I got nervous when we got to the door – because suddenly all of Kavi's warnings about cereal-killers and thieves broke into my mind. But then I remembered how Mo knew everyone and that he'd said they were nice. And I knew he'd never let me do anything dangerous.

'So I pressed the doorbell – and then when a minute had passed and nothing happened I let Kat press it too. We pressed it again, and again, and again, and Peck even pushed the letterbox open and shut at least ten times, but no one came to the door. I made a cross in my evidence book, and we walked over to the next house, which had a large white door with a golden "3" and "8" shining from it.

'This door only had a knocker, so I knocked it three times, and was just about to let Peck have a go when the door flew open and a lady with lots of bright-purple rollers in her shiny black hair and yellow rubber gloves on her hands and super-red lips popped out. Kat got shy when she saw her and hid behind my legs.

'"Yes?" she said.

'"Hello. My name's Audrey and I'm from over there," I said, pointing to my door.

'"Oh yes. You're the girl from thirty-three," said the woman. "I know you."

'"You do?" I asked. I was so surprised I looked over

my sunglasses at her. I'd definitely never seen her before. Not that I could remember anyway.

'"Of course. Say hello to your mam for me, won't you? So, what can I do for you then?"

'"Erm . . . well, I was wondering have you seen the man – or the woman, maybe – living at number forty-two?" I asked, trying to sound as nice and as unsuspicious as I could.

'But the lady's eyes narrowed and she leaned out of her door. After looking both ways like she was about to cross an invisible road, she asked, "Why?"

'"It's for a school project," I said, telling my face not to even think about going red.

'It can't have been a good answer because her eyes got even narrower and she said slowly, "No, I haven't, as it happens. Why you snooping around for a school project, anyway?"

'Thinking about it extra quick, I said we had to write about a real-life mystery for our English lesson, and that I'd chosen the mystery of who had moved in across the road. I thought it was a super-clever answer, and I think the lady believed me! Her eyes got less narrow then and she even smiled a bit. But then she said, "Ah.

Well, I can't help you even if I wanted to. I don't know who's there. If that's all then, love, I've got a wedding to get ready for, and these eyebrows aren't going to do themselves. Remember to say hello to your mam for me." And with another smile and a nod, she shut the door.

'I wrote down some notes in my evidence book and pulled Kat and Peck, who had been playing in the grass, over to the next gate. Behind it I could see the cat Mo had talked about – all gingery brown, sitting curled up on the doorstep of number forty with its eyes closed tight.

'"Kat, and Peck – now listen carefully. Stay here – and DON'T open the gate, OK? There's a cat here that's dangerous and we can't let it escape."

'Peck pressed his face against the gate immediately so that he could see it, and Kat looked curious. "Why's he dangerous?" she asked.

'"I don't know. But don't move from here, OK?" I told them.

'They both nodded, so I opened and then shut the gate extra quickly behind me, and tiptoed up to the brown wooden door with the small "40" painted on a tile next to it. I did try to be quiet and not wake the cat, but when I rang the bell it suddenly opened its eyes. In school we read about this monster woman called Medusa who had snakes in her hair and could turn you to stone if you looked in her eyes. That cat had the same kind of eyes Medusa must have had – all golden and hypnotising. I only saw them for a second before I forced my eyeballs to look away, but it was too late. The cat jumped to its feet and started hissing at me.

'It was such a horrible sound it made me turn to run away, but then the door flew open.

'"Hercules, stop that, you little brute! In you go! Go on!"

'The tall old man now standing in the doorway lifted the cat and pushed it into the house.

'"Don't mind him," he said, smiling down at me and putting his hands into his cardigan. "Thinks he owns the whole world, he does. What can I do for you, young lady?"

'I could tell he wasn't Welsh – firstly because he had a different accent, and also because no one who was Welsh would be caught dead wearing a cardi that had the Union Jack on it. But it made me remember who he was – he was Mr Bennett. Mam used to bump into him back when she was better, and he always used to say things in his funny accent like, "Jolly fine weather, eh?" and "It's AWFULLY nice to be alive, isn't it?" I hadn't seen him around for such a long time my brain had forgotten he lived on our street at all.

'"Hello," I said, pushing up my detective sunglasses. "I'm Audrey – from number thirty-three. And I'm on a school private investigation project."

'Mr Bennett nodded at me like that wasn't suspicious at all, so I asked him if he had met the person next door to him at number forty-two yet – or seen them at all.

'And then he said – exactly in this voice – let me do it for you "*Well, nooo. I can't say I haaaave. These days one doesn't like to distuuuurb the neighbours. Although I dooooo have a good mind to speak to them about that car of theirrrs – ratherrr an eyesore, don't you think?*"'

When I finish doing Mr Bennett's voice, Sergeant Anita's lips twitch and Georgie has her mouth open in surprise, so I can tell they're super impressed that I can do an English accent so well.

'It was clear Mr Bennett didn't know anything, and

I could hear Kat and Peck trying to push the gate open, so I said "Toad-in-the-hole" to him – because I think that's what people like him say when really they mean goodbye. He looked at me a bit funny, but then he said, "Yes – and do give my regards to your mother. Tell her to come by some time for tea." I made my notes again and wrote down his message for Mam too, and then we headed over to the houses on the right side of the red-door house, starting with Mrs Lumley at number forty-four.

'We rang and rang and knocked and I even said, "Hello, Mrs Lumley, it's me, Audrey!" through the letterbox, but, like at number thirty-six, no one came. Her dog wasn't barking either, which I figured meant she was definitely out. Her dog always barks at everything. So I put a cross by her door number in my evidence book, and we went over to the last house left: number forty-six.

'I think that people with new babies must have super-fast reflexes, because when I lifted Kat up to ring the doorbell for her turn, her little finger had barely pressed it for more than a second before the door opened and someone said, "Sssssssssssh!"

'At first, we couldn't see who it was – there was just a zigzaggy shadow standing in a dark hallway. But after a few seconds a man in a black T-shirt and pyjama bottoms with his hair sticking up all over his head – and something that looked like dried bird poop on his shoulder – came out into the light.

'He was so scary-looking, Kat and Peck immediately ran behind me and clung on to my legs. Now I knew why Mo had told me not to be too shocked. He looked like he had just come back from a war – except one he had fought wearing pyjamas.

'"Sorry, just got the baby down," he said, blinking as if he hadn't seen daylight in a long time. "How can I help you?"

'"My – my name's Audrey," I said super quietly. "I live at number thirty-three."

'He nodded. "Oh. Hey, Audrey. And these two – they're Kat and Peck, right?" He gave them a small wave, which made their heads go back behind my legs. "I know you guys. I'm Jahangir. Everything all right?"

'I was surprised he knew our names because we had definitely never met him before. Not unless it had been years ago when I was little. But then, how did he know who Kat and Peck were?

'"Erm . . . I'm doing a private mystery investigation for my school," I said – only a tiny bit louder so he could hear me. "And I just wanted to ask if you've ever met the person who lives at number forty-two. That's the house with the red door," I added – in case he had been indoors so long he'd forgotten what all the door numbers were.

'"No, haven't met them yet. Haven't had the time to meet anyone really," he said, scratching his head and making his hair stand up even more. "But I have seen the woman who visits."

'"What woman?" I asked, getting super excited. "What does she look like?"

'Mr Jahangir scratched his head and I could tell he was trying to think because his forehead went super wrinkly. "Well, I don't know – I've only noticed her when it's dark, see? Usually when I'm doing the night feed or changing the nappy upstairs. All I can tell you is she comes and goes through the back way. And she has hair that's in a ponytail, and she always carries a big bag – like a briefcase but for ladies."

'I quickly noted down what Mr Jahangir was saying, and then I asked, "And do you know what times she usually comes? And what time she leaves too? And does she come every night or only on some nights? And do you know what colour her hair is? And if she's tall or short? And what kind of clothes does she wear – are they black or does she wear colour? Have you seen her ever carrying any letters – like from the mail?"

'"Steady on there," said Mr Jahangir. "What is this, the Spanish Inquisition?"

'I didn't really understand why he thought I was Spanish when I clearly wasn't. So I said, "No. It's a Welsh one."

'He must have found that funny because he smiled then and said, "Ah, sorry! My mistake." Then he started answering my questions, ticking them off one by one on his hands. "No, I don't know the exact times she comes or leaves – and I'm not sure if it's every night. I've only seen her once or twice. We're up when our son's up, and that's different every night." He sighed. "Hmm, what else did you ask? Her hair? I think it's brown . . . and she's average height, and wears just normal clothes, I think – though she always has a white cardi on," he added. "Was that all your questions?"

'"The mail – have you seen her carrying any letters – or maybe, a ninja bottle?"

'Mr Jahangir frowned then and said slowly, "Er . . . noooo. Why?"

'"No reason," I said, finishing my notes quickly. "Thanks a lot!"

'"You're welcome," said Mr Jahangir. And then he said, "Take care, guys. And say hi to your mam for me. Tell her me and my wife and me mam send her our regards too."

'I was going to ask him how he knew Mam, but before I could say anything else he had disappeared into his dark hall again and shut the door.

'After I got home, I spent the afternoon with Mam and told her I'd got everything I needed for my homework project and I gave her all the messages the neighbours had given to me for her. I wanted to ask her how they all knew who we were, but she was in pain and gave me her "I'm-too-tired-no-more-questions-please" look, so I reminded myself to ask when she was feeling better.

'Just before bed that night, I went over all my new notes. I had so much to share with Inara and Kavi on Monday, and I knew they'd be super excited I had found out so much. But the truth was, I now had even more questions than I had started with – like who exactly was the woman who went in and out of number forty-two in the middle of the night? And how come everyone knew who me and Mam and Kat and Peck were? Had they met us all before? And if they had, why couldn't *I* remember them? And why did Mam not seem even a bit surprised when I'd told her the neighbours had all had messages for her? I don't know what happens in a Spanish inquisition, but my Welsh one had left me feeling more confused than ever. And I had the feeling Mam knew something about our neighbours that I didn't – something she didn't want to share with me.'

# 6

## The Doctor's Orders

'And what happened after your inquiries, Audrey? Did you find out who the lady was? The one your neighbour at . . .' Sergeant Anita looks down at her notes, 'number forty-six saw in the night? Was it she who made you want to travel down here?'

'A bit, I guess,' I explain. 'Because when I heard about her, it made me feel like my suspicions were right – about *Them* being there to spy on us. In the documentary I saw with Mam, the social services spies sat up all night in the dark eating sandwiches and noodles and looking through binoculars – and I figured someone had to bring them all that food, so I guessed this lady was doing that for the spy across the street. So I knew if it really was *Them*, I had to act even harder like we were normal and keep Mam away from the windows. But all the things that started happening *after* made it harder and harder for me to pretend like everything was OK, and harder and harder for me to hide what was happening, which is sort of what led to me coming here.

'That week – and that weekend – was the last good week Mam had. She even managed to walk to the corner shop and back again that Sunday – the day after my inquisition, which made me think that maybe her bones might be getting stronger.

'But then, two days later, everything started going all horrible – and got worse than ever before.

'In my class diary on Monday, I wrote all about meeting the neighbours and how funny the woman in the curlers and Mr Bennett and Mr Jahangir were. Only I pretended that I was posting them an invitation for tea and Welsh cakes at my house, instead of me knocking on their doors to ask questions – just so Mrs Li didn't think I was strange. And in all the break times that day, and on Tuesday too, me and Inara and Kavi tried to figure out who the midnight woman might be. I showed them my evidence book, which I had decided to call "The Welsh Inquisition Book" instead, and they helped me put more questions in it that I hadn't thought of. Questions to ask Mam too – because they said she might have seen things while I was at school, or she might know of another neighbour I should ask. We still hadn't heard back about our message in the ninja bottle, but that didn't seem so important any more. Not when we knew there was a back gate and a mysterious woman that needed spying on instead.

'But then that Tuesday afternoon I got home to find Mam had started having a Nightmare Day while I had been away. She was super sick and in agony all that night. By dawn she was in so much pain that I had to call Dr Adeola on his private phone and beg him to come and see her right away – just in case she'd injured herself anywhere and he could help. You see, because Mam's bones hurt so much anyway, she can't tell if she's got a fracture or something – because the pain of that would just get covered up by her everyday pains.

'Dr Adeola said he would come straight after his first patient and that he'd get to us by ten. So I did what I always do when I know he's coming to visit. I tidied the whole house, and I woke up Kat and Peck and got them ready and, after I said hi and bye to Mo, I ran with them to school just as fast as I could. On Mam's Doctor Days, I always drop Kat and Peck off at a tree around the corner from the entrance to school so no one sees me. From there, I tell them to run as fast as they can into their classroom, and I run as fast as I can back to Mam. I know it's not good – me not going to school on school days, but it'd be worse if Peck and Kat had to bunk too. I only make them do it when Mam is so bad I can't leave the house at all. That day was bad, but her screams weren't as bad as some of the other times. So it was OK for me to leave her for ten minutes exactly.

'When I got back I waited with Mam, and sat next to her and told her to breathe and not to give up. I gave her water through a straw whenever she needed it, and tried to get her to watch telly so she could take her mind off what her body was doing. But the pain was so bad her eyes were squeezed shut. Then, after what felt like forty hours but was really only one, I heard Dr Adeola's knock on our door. His knock goes *TAP-TAP, TAP-TAP, TAP!* like a Morse code that's not finished yet.

'I ran down and opened the door to him, and he said, "Hello, Audrey. Clearly Mam's not had enough apples today, eh?" He always says that when he visits us, and it always makes me smile. Even when I'm scared.

'"How are you doing?" he asked. "You OK?"

'I nodded and shrugged at the same time, wondering what it might be like to have Dr Adeola as a tad. He was always so nice. His children were super lucky.

'"Is she downstairs today?" he asked.

'I shook my head and led him straight up to her room.

'"Thank you, darling . . . that's all," said Mam, gritting her teeth and trying not to show the doctor – or me – just how much pain she was in.

'Whenever Mam says those five words, it means I have to leave and go and wait somewhere quietly until Dr Adeola is done. But I only pretended to leave. I closed the door and walked off loudly, but then I crept back and listened from outside. I've been doing that for years, because Mam never tells me everything. Dropping eaves isn't a crime . . . is it? Not when you need to know if your mam is going to be OK?'

I stop speaking to make sure it isn't. Sergeant Anita shakes her head and gives me a small smile. 'No. I think that rule only really applies when there are state secrets involved. Don't worry Audrey. Please go on.'

'Good . . . well, I'm glad I listened at the door. Even though what I heard started me thinking all the thoughts that led me . . . well, *here*,' I say, looking around at the room.

'Why's that?' asks Sergeant Anita, while Georgie looks at me with wide eyes. 'What did you hear?'

'I heard everything the doctor ordered. Usually Mam tells Dr Adeola that she needs stronger medicine to help her not be in pain any more. And usually Dr Adeola looks through her records to see what he can swap or make stronger. But this time he sounded worried – which made me feel worried too. He said, "I can't keep upping your meds like this, Maya!" Maya's my mam's name – isn't it the prettiest name? Then he said, "At some point it's simply not going to be enough, and I think we're reaching that point fast. You've got away without all the things I've been suggesting long enough, but we need to get ahead of the curve now. You need an electric wheelchair if you want to go to the shops. Trying to walk up and down kerbs and all our hills carrying things – even if it's just to the corner shop – isn't going to do, not any more. And at some point you're either going to have to move downstairs and get an accessible bathroom, or have an en suite built upstairs. And you definitely need a stairlift. You can't be moving up and down the stairs five, six times a day. What do you think would happen if there was ever a fire, or an emergency with one of the kids? We need to make your life as fully accessible as possible. The longer you leave it all, the more days of pain it'll lead to – and worse pain too. The tablets can only do so much, and *you* can only take so much! I'm sorry. I know it isn't easy to hear. But I'm going to have to get strict now. I have to. For your own good, for your own *life*."

'I could hear Mam sad-crying through the door. She doesn't like to cry, so when she does, I know it's serious. Her sad-cry is different from her pain-cry, and in some ways it's much, much worse. In fact, I think it's one of the worst sounds on the planet – even worse than nails screeching on a blackboard or cats fighting in the dark. The only good thing about Mam's sad-cry is it never lasts longer than a minute.

'When she was finished, I heard her ask, "And how am I supposed to get all those things, Doc? We don't have any money coming in from anywhere, so I can't buy them. You know our situation. And we both know the NHS is on its knees. I've heard how long all the waiting lists are. It'll be months, maybe years, before they get to me. Might even be never if the ones down in Westminster get their way and sell us all off to the highest bidder. They don't care about anyone else but their own, and they certainly don't care about the likes of me. They'll just keep on pretending we don't exist."

'Then Dr Adeola said, "There are ways, Maya. It'll be tough, I won't lie. It might be months, maybe even over a year. But we've got to try. The thing is, I can't do anything if you don't agree in the first place. Do it for the kids. Do it for me and save me from getting mad and tamping! A wheelchair will help you get out and about more easily – you could even head down to the beach on your good days. Get on a bus and go see friends. I know the kids dream of going out with you properly – the little 'uns haven't ever had that with you really, have they?"

'Mam didn't say anything – or if she did, I couldn't hear her – but she must have nodded because then I heard Dr Adeola say, "Good! Let me get started on my end of things, and I'll send through some paperwork for you to look at – grants and things that might help. Get Audrey to help you. I know how golden she is."

'It felt nice hearing Dr Adeola say I was "golden". It made me want to help Mam even more. So after he told Mam what to do with her medicines and left, I asked her if she wanted me to move her things downstairs. She knew I'd dropped eaves all over the place, but she didn't say anything about it. She just shook her head slowly and said, "No, darling. Not yet. I don't think me sleeping on the sofa right now is going to help anyone. It's too cold downstairs at the moment – maybe when the weather gets warmer. But I'll spend as much time as I can down there. Promise."

'I could tell right away that Mam wasn't going to listen to the doctor's orders all the way – not until she didn't have a choice left. It made me feel angry. But I also knew she would hate sleeping in our living room. It was only a small square and it was filled with Kat and Peck's toys, and old books, and a sofa that was so old and hard we preferred sitting on the floor anyway.

'That night I couldn't sleep because of all the worries swimming around in my head. Everything Dr Adeola had ordered was too expensive – and what if Mam was right and the applications and hospitals took too long? Or even worse, what if they *never* helped us? I didn't know who she meant by the people in the West Minister place – but it sounded like they were people who cared more about making money than helping people. And the harder I thought, the more I realised there was no one who could help us get everything Mam needed. We didn't know anyone who was a bajillionaire, and my grandparents weren't alive any more, and Mam didn't have any brothers or sisters, so I didn't have aunts or uncles I could call like other people did.

'It had to be me.

'I was the only one who could get her all the things she needed and stop her from worrying about all the money we didn't have. She was too proud to ask for help, but I wasn't. I do everything I can to make her life better every single day, even when that sometimes means being a – a criminal. I'm going to tell you about that too, I promise . . .

'So if a wheelchair and a sweet bathroom and a lift for the stairs was what Mam needed, then that's exactly what I promised myself I would get for her. No matter what I had to do, or who I had to ask for help.'

# 7

## The Other Shoebox

I look up at Georgie and Sergeant Anita and fall quiet for a few seconds.

'Everything OK, Audrey? Do you need a break – maybe some water?' asks Georgie.

I shake my head. 'No. It's just . . . I have to tell you about something I did – after that day. I just . . . I *had* to do it – there was no other way. The only thing is, I – I don't want Mam to find out. You won't tell her, will you? It's just – if she found out, she'd be even more upset than she already is, and that might make her more ill, and I think if she knew about everything I've done she might . . . hate me forever.'

Sergeant Anita and Georgie stay quiet for a few seconds, before Sergeant Anita clears her throat.

'I think, Audrey, that whatever action you felt you had to take would be understood by a great many people. Including your mam. It is really important that you go on telling the truth and explaining what happened, so that we can judge how best to help anyone who might have been . . . impacted by your actions.'

'And you won't tell Mam?' I ask.

'Not her unless we have to,' says Sergeant Anita.

It isn't the answer I want, but it makes me feel a bit better somehow. Maybe after I tell them everything, if they *have* to tell Mam about it, they can make her understand that I didn't ever mean to become what I am, and that sometimes it's the world that makes you into things, even when they're the last things you ever want to be.

'OK . . .' I sit up in my chair, and tell myself and the grey sack in my hand that I won't stop until I feel as empty as a hoover that's just been cleaned out – no matter how dusty and dirt-covered all my secrets are.

'After I made up my mind to get Mam everything she needed for the doctor's orders, I tried to think of what I could do to afford them,' I explained. 'I knew we needed thousands of pounds – electric wheelchairs and getting a whole bathroom and a stairlift would probably cost more than everything we owned all put together. So I made a list of all the things I might try in the back of my evidence book. They included . . .'

I squeeze my eyes shut and use my fingers to help me remember how many ideas I'd written out. It was definitely five.

'The first was playing the lottery. But for that idea, I'd need to know someone who was old enough to get the tickets for me. I thought maybe Mo could help. But then I'd still need money to buy the tickets in the first place, and what if I played and played and never won?

'The second was doing a bake sale. Amitav in year six did one last year and he raised nearly three hundred pounds to save the snow leopards! But then I remembered my roast chicken catching on fire. Plus baking ingredients cost loads of money, and there's the gas bill too, so I couldn't do that either.

'The third was doing a sponsored run. But I couldn't think of anyone who would sponsor me thousands of pounds to run in Swansea. It's so small there aren't many places to run to and it's raining half the time anyway. That's probably why we don't have an

Abertawe marathon that's famous like the London and New York ones.

'The fourth was breaking into the house opposite to see if there really *were* diamonds hidden there, like Kavi said, and getting a reward from the police and the jewellery shop. But then I realised there might not be anything there at all and I could get caught by the robbers instead. Or, if Kavi was wrong and I was right and it was *Them*, then they might catch me and take me away. I couldn't risk it.

'And then I thought of my final idea . . .

'Tad.

'I thought, maybe he might not be as lost as Mam made out. And if I found him, and spoke to him, he could help us. He would have to, once he found out how bad things were. He was definitely rich enough – I knew that because of all the gifts he got us at Christmas. In the last box there had been a brand-new pair of roller blades that were just my size, and a rucksack filled with all the books I had been wanting to read but were always checked out from the school library – and the monster trucks and Lego sets Kat had been wanting, and art kits and the exact trainers Peck had been asking for all year. In fact, it had every single thing we had asked for on our Christmas wish lists. Mo posted them out to "Santa Claus, The North Pole" for us every year, and every year since Tad had left us they had come true. I knew it wasn't actually Santa who brought us the gifts because they always got delivered *before* Christmas Day. So I figured it must be Mam secretly telling Tad what we wanted, and him getting all the things for us, even though she always said she didn't ever want anything from him.

'I decided right away that idea number five was the best idea. All I needed to do was find out where Tad had gone, get his address or phone number and ask him to help Mam.

'The next day, when I wasn't looking after Kat and Peck, and I wasn't busy acting like everything was OK back at school, I started my search. Mam has a little book where she keeps important information written down, and I was pretty sure Tad's details would be inside it. She keeps it by her bed, so I slipped it out of her room that night when she was sleeping and looked through every page. I knew my tad's name: it was Dylan Hughes. But his name wasn't in there at all.

'Next, I had to check her phone. I managed to do that while Mam was slowly helping Kat and Peck get cleaned and changed into their pyjamas. I knew the password because I'm her emergency everything, so once I was in I went to her contacts and then typed in D and then D-Y and then D-Y-L-A-N.

'But nothing showed up.

'Then I wondered if maybe she had a nickname for him. I knew it probably wasn't a nice nickname because he left us after the loudest argument ever and when Mam was really ill. So I tried all the different things I remembered her calling him whenever they used to fight. But I couldn't find "FART HEAD" or "BUCKET FACE" on her phone either.

'At school, I didn't tell Kavi or Inara what Dr Adeola had said. Everyone was getting worried about all the pretend tests Mrs Li said we had to do to get ready for the real tests after Easter holidays – those are next week you know! – and all the homework she had started giving us. I didn't really care about the exams and tests and things. I mean, I don't want to be at the bottom of the class, and I do want to be a doctor and help make my mam's pains go away, so I do listen to

Mrs Li and try my best. But the truth is, even if I did the best in everything, I can't ever leave Mam or Swansea. So my grades don't matter that much. I was glad Inara and Kavi and Nutan and everyone was so busy and worried about them though. It gave me more time to think about how I could find my tad's address. I had searched nearly all of Mam's room whenever she wasn't in it and still hadn't found anything.

'It wasn't until Friday – just three days after Dr Adeola had made his orders, that I got a new idea of where I might find it – and it was all thanks to Mo. He gave me a stamp, see – it'd been sent all the way from New York City. And on it were three women running in a race with bright-silver trainers on. As soon as I saw the trainers, something in my brain snapped its fingers – and I remembered a shoebox, just like the one I hide my stamps in. Only the shoebox in my memory was much, much older. I had seen it years ago – just after Tad had left. It had been filled with letters and dried flowers and old photos and Mam had told me to put it away and to never touch it again. I never had, but I was sure that inside it were letters from my tad that might have his address on them.

'I had to wait until Sunday morning to get the chance to search Mam's room again without her in it, but the second I did, I looked super fast. I found the box inside an old plastic bag right at the back of her wardrobe, and the second I saw it I could just feel it would have what I was looking for. Sneaking it to my room, I took off the elastic band that was keeping the lid on and looked inside. It was like a treasure chest filled with crispy paper and ink and library-book smells. Right on the top of everything was an envelope with Mam's name and our address and a faded golden stamp on it. And underneath the address, at the bottom of the envelope, were the words:

For Audrey, Kat and Peck.

<u>PLEASE MAKE SURE THEY GET THIS ONE DAY</u>

'The last words were underlined and all in capitals . . . see?'

Sergeant Anita and Georgie watch as I put my hand in my front dungarees pocket and take out a crinkled, folded envelope. I put it on the table in front of me.

'Do you mind if I read what's inside, Audrey?' asks Sergeant Anita.

I don't, so I hold the envelope out to her and watch as she carefully takes out the sheet of paper and reads it silently. With an 'Ah' she shows it to Georgie, and then places it back in the envelope.

'Thank you for sharing that with us. It's a very short message . . .' she says.

'Yeah,' I say, quietly, ignoring the sad look in her eyes. 'But that didn't matter. All that was important was the envelope. Because on the back there was an address. *His* address. And that was all *I* needed to help get Mam everything *she* needed.'

# 8

## The Invitations

'What did you decide to do once you had the address?' asks Sergeant Anita, handing Tad's envelope back to me.

I place it carefully back in my dungarees pocket, right next to where I can feel my heart beating.

'I was going to write to him that day, but then almost the second after I finished reading Tad's words, Mam called me downstairs. I hid the shoebox under my bed and went to help her. But Mam was only calling me because she said I had to revise – one of the pretend exams were the next day, and she knew I was nervous about them. I told her they didn't matter and that I could revise properly over the holidays for the real ones, but she said she wasn't having any of it. She tried to help me go over questions in the workbooks Mrs

Li had given us while we got Kat and Peck ready for bed, but there were too many thoughts going around in my head, so I stopped answering after a while. She told me to go straight to bed and rest my brain then, but it felt like my brain was running on a treadmill. I think Mam saying even the pretend exams mattered had started to make me feel panicky.

'The next day, I couldn't think about anything else except the exams. Everyone looked well green and sick when we finished – even Vijayarani, who's always the best in everything. When the bell rang for break time and Mrs Li took in all our exam papers, she ordered us to go outside and play as hard as we could until the colour came back to our cheeks.

'And we were doing just that when a super-strange thing happened. Actually, two super-strange things happened that day – the first one was right there in the playground. And the second one happened after I got home from school.

'The first thing was that Fatima and Carey and Fred came up to me and Inara and Kavi and Angie and Larry. We'd all been standing in a line doing the car-wash competition and—'

'Sorry, Audrey. What's a car-wash competition?' asks Georgie.

I stare back at her and realise she's never heard of that game either! Life sure is sad and boring for grown-ups. It makes me hope I'll never become one. Not on the inside anyway.

'It's where you pretend to be one of the balloon men at the car wash that are all wavy and go up and down. Like this,' I say, jumping down from the police-station chair. Holding on to the grey sack, I begin wriggling and shaking my legs and body and waving my arms and bending down and coming back up again. 'See?'

Sergeant Anita suddenly looks like she's accidentally swallowed cough medicine, and Georgie pats her chest and with a 'Huh-Hm!' says, 'I had no idea that was a game.'

'Yeah, it's real cool,' I say, sitting back down. 'You see who can go lowest and then the tallest, and whoever does, wins.'

'So you say you were playing this game, when three children approached you?' asks Sergeant Anita, her face looking normal again.

'Yup. Fatima, Carey and Fred,' I say slowly, because

I could see Sergeant Anita writing their names down. 'We stopped playing right away when they came up to us, because Fatima is one of the coolest girls in the whole of Wales. Her father plays for the Welsh rugby team, so everyone wants to be her friend, but nobody ever really gets to be except Carey and Fred. She's in the class next door and she definitely isn't friends with me or Kavi or Inara so when she came walking up to us, we didn't know what to do.

'Kavi opened his mouth to say something but instead he burped and turned bright orange. Usually Inara would have laughed at him, but she was too busy staring up at Fatima with her mouth open, and trying to stop her cat headband from slipping off her head.

'At first I didn't think Fatima had come to speak to us at all and that she'd made a mistake, but then she flicked her extra-shiny long black plait over her shoulder, and held up some purple envelopes like they were playing cards and she was a magician.

'"Are you guys Audrey . . . Inara . . . Kavi . . . and Angie and Larry?" asked Fatima, reading our names off the envelopes.

'I nodded shyly. Angie must have been super nervous

like Kavi, because she suddenly giggled like the Joker in the *Batman* cartoons and then made a loud snorting sound and went quiet. And Larry nodded as if his head had turned into a bobble-head toy.

'"You're all invited to my birthday party," Fatima said, throwing an envelope out to each of us like frisbees. "Don't be late. And follow all the instructions or you won't be allowed in. 'Kay?"

'"Yeah!" said Fred, making his ears wiggle up and down. Fred is famous for being the only boy in school who can make his ears wiggle independently of each other. Mr Garcia says he's going to be one of the richest people in Swansea when he grows up, because he's already started making lots of money by getting people to pay to watch him move them.

'"And don't dress *lame*!" added Carey. "All the teachers in school, including Mr Garcia, are coming too." Then she gave Fred a thump on the arm, before following Fatima back into the screams of the playground.

'None of us said a word for about three seconds, and then we all started ripping open our envelopes. Fatima had a huge birthday party every year and they were always legend! Everyone across Wales talked about them for weeks and weeks after. One year the national news covered her party – because the pony that people were taking turns riding on broke free and went galloping out on to the motorway. Inara and me had never ever been invited to one. Kavi had – but only because his parents knew her parents, and he said there might be a world war if he didn't get invited. He always snuck Inara and me lots of sweets and gift bags and things, but it wasn't the same as actually going.

'I ripped my special envelope open and watched as a sparkling shower of bright-green glitter sprinkled all over my clothes. Inara growled – her school jumper was covered with it too. I pulled out the invitation. It had animals all around the sides holding balloons, and a ringmaster holding up a banner with the words "You are invited to . . ."

'The rest of the invitation said Fatima's birthday party was going to be circus-themed, and was going to take place at her house on Mumbles beach on Saturday – that's the Saturday just gone, you know. And that if I wanted to go, I had to be dropped off by my parents at exactly three o'clock, and picked up again "no later than seven p.m.". And that the dress code was "sparkly circus extravaganza".

'Kavi was super excited and yelled "TIDY!" and Angie and Larry jumped and skipped on the spot, completely forgetting they were meant to try and look cool.

'"I bet I know why she's inviting us all of a sudden," said Inara. "It's because Mr Garcia and Mrs Li would notice if we weren't there. Ugh. I *almost* don't want to go . . ."

'"Yeah, totally," I said. I couldn't really say anything else because there was an invisible hard-boiled egg stuck in my chest. If Mrs Li was going, and Mr Garcia was going, then that meant I would need to go to the party too – to show them I was normal. And that meant finding the right clothes to wear – and getting to the house in Mumbles somehow . . . and pretending Mam had just dropped me off . . . and getting a present that was as good as everyone else's presents . . . and leaving my house for more than twenty minutes.

'By home-time, everyone in school had forgotten all about the exams and how to do our times tables and write full sentences. All anyone could talk about was who was going to Fatima's party and what they were going to wear. The excitement was even more electric because of Mr Garcia being invited. He'd never been to any of the other parties, and so everyone wanted to show off and have the best costumes and presents. I tried to join in and act like I was excited too, but the hard-boiled egg in my chest wouldn't budge. It always turned up whenever there was something I really, really wanted to do, but I knew I couldn't.

'Getting that invitation from Fatima was the first strange thing to happen that day.

'The second thing was waiting for me when I got home.

'That afternoon, we got in to find Mam in the kitchen. The extra medicines Dr Adeola had given her seemed to be working because she hadn't had any more Nightmare Days, and that day she was making us sandwiches for tea, which meant she was feeling OK. I love Mam's sandwiches – she makes them extra slowly because of her hands, and for some reason, that makes them taste much nicer. I went over to help her and told her all about Fatima's party invitation and how much I wanted to go. She smiled and said, "Let's see," which made me so happy I gave her a cwtch. And then she pointed to something next to the bread bin.

'"Oh, and that came for you this morning," she said. "Mo brought it by after he finished his rounds. He said it'd been left on the doorstep across the road for you."

'I couldn't believe it. It was the water bottle – Kavi's ninja turtles water bottle! And it had something inside it!

'"The instructions are there, see," said Mam, pointing at the bright-yellow Post-it note on one side of the bottle. I tried not to notice that her hands were shaking a little bit and read the label instead. It said:

DEAR MR POSTMAN.
PLEASE DELIVER THIS TO
THE GIRL AT NUMBER 33.

'It was written out in wonky, shaky letters – as if it had been written by someone Kat and Peck's age. They always wrote in capitals too because they said they were easier to remember than the smaller letters.

'I took off the lid and turned it upside down. A rolled-up note fell out, along with a two-pound coin, which spun around on its tip on the counter until it came to a stop. The note said:

PLEASE WASH THE CAR
WHEN CONVENIENT.
TIP ENCLOSED. THANK YOU.

'It made me so surprised I cried out "MAM! They want me to wash their car – for REAL!"

'Mam asked me who it was, and when I told her I had been trying to make friends with the new neighbour across the street, she said it looked like my plan had worked.

'But then that made me think, what if this was a part of *Their* plan? What if it was a trap? And why had it taken so long for them to write back? What if *They* had spent all that time coming up with something to get me closer to the house so they could find out more things about us?

'I picked up the golden coin. It was the first time

since my grandparents had died that I had been given any money that wasn't for groceries or bills. But it wasn't just mine, it was Inara and Kavi's too. I was staring down at it wondering what to do, when I heard Mam say, "Oh come on! There must be something else in the house . . ."

'I looked up and saw Mam searching for things to give to us for tea. She found an old packet of Rich Tea biscuits and, shaking her head, slowly placed one on each of our plates, next to our jam sandwiches. I looked at the bread packet and realised we only had a couple of slices left, and barely any butter. I'd seen Mam pretend she wasn't hungry loads of times so that there'd be food for me and Kat and Peck. I had been so busy with the house across the street and doctor's orders and the exams, I hadn't realised it was that time of the month again. I should have guessed sooner, because of all the white envelopes Mo had been delivering all week – the ones that had nothing inside them except bills. I hate those white envelopes. They eat and gobble all of Mam's money like big fat caterpillars that make holes in everything. Including hearts. But the worst thing is, I can't help her when they arrive. Not even one little bit. I still have to wait seven whole years before I can get money to help. Being nine means I don't count as a "Young Carer" yet, even though I'm young and I do care for Mam just as much as I can.

'There was only one solution. I had to become the one thing I knew how to be without anyone ever teaching me: and that was a lifter criminal.'

# 9

## The Shoplifter's Guide to the Galaxy

'Can – can I have some water now? Or some squash?' I ask, my throat feeling dry.

'Of course,' says Sergeant Anita. 'Would you like something to eat too? You've been travelling all day.'

'We can get you some sandwiches and crisps?' suggests Georgie.

I shake my head. I'm not hungry at all. Just thirsty. Sergeant Anita goes to the door and says something to someone outside.

'That'll be here in two ticks,' she says, giving me a smile.

'You're doing really well, Audrey,' says Georgie, placing her ring-covered hand on my arm and giving it a tap. 'Really, *really* well.'

I wonder if she'll still think that in a few minutes when I tell them the next part of what I did. Probably not. By the time I've finished telling them everything, I bet they'll be super glad they caught me and decide they *do* want to press charges and put me in jail.

We wait silently, until another police officer knocks and then walks into the room carrying a plastic cup of orange squash. He's so tall and straight he moves like a ruler.

'Thank you,' says Sergeant Anita as he puts my cup down, one hand behind his back like a butler. 'That'll be all.'

'Ma'am!' he says, before walking stiffly back out and closing the door behind him.

I take a long sip of the orange squash and feel it gush down my throat like a waterfall and land in the lake of my tummy.

'Do all prisoners get served orange squash?' I ask, wondering why it tastes so nice and different to the squash we have at home.

Sergeant Anita looks surprised. 'No,' she replies. 'Only members of the public who deserve it. And as I said before, Audrey, you're not a prisoner! This isn't a jail, it's just an interview room, and you're being interviewed, that's all.'

'I know,' I say. 'Still, it's really nice squash.'

'Ready to go on?' asks Sergeant Anita.

I nod because I am.

'You were saying something about being a "lifter criminal"?' she reminds me. 'What do you mean by that?'

I fall silent for a few seconds and look at the door, wishing I could run right through it and disappear. But I'm not a coward, so I take a deep breath and start again. 'This next bit is the bit Mam can't know about. Not ever.'

Sergeant Anita and Georgie don't say anything. They just look at me and give me *OK* looks with their eyes.

'Sometimes . . . when lots of bills come in, Mam – well, she doesn't have enough money left from what she gets from the government people for our food. It always happens around the same time of the month, and it really worries her and stops her sleeping too. I can always tell when it's coming because Mo starts bringing us lots of thin white envelopes that only have bills inside them. Have you ever noticed how those envelopes are so stingy that they don't even come with real stamps on them – just ink and circles in the corner? They take so much money from people, you'd think they could at least buy stamps!

'Well, one time – when I was about seven – it got so bad that I – I started borrowing things to help us stop starving. And I've done it a few times since then too. Maybe more than a few times,' I admit. 'But I only do it when I really *really* have to – it's not all the time, I promise.'

I look down at the table and speak the next part to it. Sometimes it's easier to tell the truth when you don't have to look at something with eyes.

'So the next day – after the day when Fatima invited us all to her party and the car-wash invite came and Mam didn't have any tea for herself – I woke up super early. On days when I know I have to be a lifter, I wake up a whole hour earlier than everyone else, see. That morning was dark and there were lots of grey rain clouds in the sky, hovering around like angry-looking spaceships. I was glad it was cold and miserable – rainy weather makes what I have to do easier.

'First, I checked Mam was asleep – sometimes her painkillers don't work and she just lies awake or wanders around her room even before the sun's up. But I could hear her nose whistling so I knew she was having a good sleep for once. When Mam's sleeping she sounds like someone who's trying to play the recorder but who can't blow it hard enough to make a real note. It's one of my favourite sounds.

'I left her door half open, and I checked on Kat and Peck. They were lying with their arms and legs flung all over each other, just like two starfish that had got tangled up by an ocean wave. They look so cute when they sleep like that. I checked the clock in their room, and I remember it being six fifty-four a.m. exactly. That meant I had thirty-six minutes before anyone started missing me.

'I pulled my biggest hoodie and coat on over my pyjamas, and grabbed Mam's purse, my keys and Peck's dinosaur watch. I don't have a watch myself, and timing is really important for criminals like me.

'I never wanted to be a criminal,' I add, wanting Sergeant Anita and George to know that before I carry on any further. 'I kind of just turned into one. When Tad left us and Mam had to give up her job, I realised that having nearly no money meant having nearly no food, and I couldn't help it. I'm pretty sure I wasn't a criminal when I was a baby, but maybe I took things that weren't mine all the time – like treats and toys and baby formula. But even if I wasn't then, I definitely am now. Especially because my nose is super stiff.'

'Your nose?' asks Sergeant Anita, making me look up at her.

Nodding, I put my finger on my nose and press down. 'See?' I say, showing her and feeling sad. 'It's so hard it doesn't even go down any more. It never used to be like that. I think it means I'm a hard-nosed criminal now, like the ones the newsreaders are always talking about.'

Sergeant Anita closes her eyes and stays really still – as if she's trying to stop herself from sneezing. And Georgie's looking over at me with her lips shut so tight they've disappeared.

I wait, wondering if both of them need some water or something. But then Sergeant Anita says, 'I see . . . Go on,' and Georgie nods too.

'The thing is, I don't lift banks or jewellery stores and trains or anything like that. I've never lifted a diamond or a car or taken even a penny of money – so

I'm not a criminal-criminal. I only take things that will stop Mam and me and Kat and Peck from going hungry.

'The first time I became a shoplifter, I didn't even know what I was doing. I'll never forget that day. Mam had sent me get some medicine from the pharmacy. I'd run straight there and was waiting for the chemist to get everything from the back bit of the pharmacy where all the medicines are. I was just looking around and thinking about school when I saw a long row of shiny chocolate bars wrapped in gold on the counter. They were the brand-new SHOUT! bars. *Everyone* at school had been talking about them – mostly because inside some of the wrappers were prizes, and you could win a lifetime of free bars if you were lucky. I hadn't tried one yet because they were way more expensive than the supermarket chocolate bars, which Mam only let us buy on very special occasions anyway, and I was desperate to taste one. So before I even knew what they were doing, my eyes swivelled around like they had turned into CCTV cameras, and after they checked there was no one inside the shop with me, my fingers quickly shoved a bar into my coat pocket! My face must have gone super red because I felt a huge rush of fire travel right up from my feet to my hair as if I was ready for lift-off, but before I could make myself put the chocolate bar back, the chemist had come back out and was giving me Mam's bag of tablets and oils.

'I don't think I've ever hurried out of a shop as quickly as I did that day. I felt so horrible and sick and worried that she had seen me and was going to call the police – and maybe the SHOUT! chocolate bar people too so that they'd never give me a prize even if I did get a winning bar. I promised myself that one day, when I had my own money, I would pay her back.

'I still feel guilty about stealing that chocolate bar – I feel guilty every time I have to lift something. But the next day at school, when I pulled that bar out of my pocket in front of Kavi and Inara, Inara got so excited she shouted out to everyone that I had one. Before I knew it, half the playground had gathered all around me to see if my wrapper had a prize inside it. It didn't, but I'll never forget how my chest got tingly and jumpy because I felt normal. Like I was doing something everyone else got to do every day but I never usually did.

'Ever since that day, I've kept count of all the money

I owe to all the shops I've had to lift things from. I keep all the numbers in a tiny black book inside my box of stamps. Sometimes I have nightmares about someone finding it and showing it to Mam, and me getting arrested by the Welsh FBI, and being sent to the dungeons in a castle hidden so deep in the Welsh valleys that no one ever finds me again . . .

'That thought always scares me – everyone finding out . . .

'I have tried to stop lifting things. After that first chocolate bar, I promised myself I would never, ever, *ever* take anything from anyone ever again. But then things kept on getting more and more expensive – the bills and the rent and food too. Mam always puts as much money aside for our food as she can every month, but we can't get the same amount of food for that money like we used to. So I take the things we need but can't really afford. Like the nice butter that Mam likes and not the one that comes in a tub and tastes like plastic, and the biscuits that Kat and Peck want, and the small cartons of the extra-creamy milk and yoghurt to help Mam's bones grow stronger. And fruit too. One time I managed to take seven bananas in one go. But my record has been taking a whole pack of burgers, buns, a bottle of ketchup and a tin of custard without getting caught! I'll never forget how happy Mam and Kat and Peck were when I made the burgers for tea, and served the custard with a heated-up chocolate bar so it was all gooey and crunchy at the same time.

'Mam sometimes asks me how we've been able to afford some of the food, and I have to lie. That's the other horrible thing about being a criminal – all the lying you have to do so you don't get caught by the people you love. I tell her that I find things half-price when she sends me shopping on my own. Or when I lift biscuits and sweets, I tell her that Inara and Kavi did swaps with me at lunchtime at school.

'It's not easy being a criminal, so I'm hoping that when my tad comes and helps us, I can stop. I hate going into a shop knowing that I have to lift something. Every time I have to do it, my heart leaves my chest and sits right at the back of my throat and I can hear it beating everywhere. And when the perfect moment to take something comes, my hands and feet go as cold as frozen fish fingers and everything stops. Even the galaxy feels like it's stopped spinning to see if I'm going to make it. Sometimes I feel as if I'm not even the one being the criminal, that the real me is hovering in the air, watching from above as someone else who only *looks* like me lifts things.

'I guess I must be good at being a criminal, because in all the time I've been taking things, I've only ever been caught twice. The very first time was when I tried to take three cans of soup under my jumper and they all fell out just as I reached the supermarket doors. Luckily the security guard let go of my arm the second I started to cry and I managed to run away.

'The second time was at the Christmas market in town last year. I tried to lift a mini Christmas tree – the kind that people put on their desks, you know – for Kat and Peck because we hadn't had a Christmas tree in so long. I hid it under my coat, but it had bells on it and jingled when I moved. I got arrested by the shop police and they nearly called my mam. But then for some reason, the officer let me go – and he let me take the tree home too! I don't know why, but I guess he must have felt sorry for me. We still have the tree. It's on top of the mantlepiece in the living room.

'There isn't a guidebook about how to get things

when you don't have enough money and even your mam can't help you, so I've made up my own rules. I've got three giant rules I try to never ever break, and five smaller rules that I break only if I have to, and they help me not get caught.

'That morning last week I didn't know how bad things were going to get. If I had, I'd have just stayed in bed. But I didn't, so after I put on Peck's dinosaur watch I slipped out of the door and ran to the shops at the bottom of my road. I was a regular at all of them, and I knew exactly which one I was going to lift from – Mrs Davies' shop. Even though it's not as big as the mini supermarket next door, Mrs Davies' has everything you could ever need – and her shop doubles up as a Post Office too. I decided to go there because I could get what I needed not just for our fridge at home but for Fatima's birthday too. Plus, Mrs Davies is almost as blind as a bat; even though she wears huge glasses that are as thick as a slice of bread, she can still barely see anything.

'At first, everything went fine. I went into Mrs Davies' shop like normal, and the door made its usual *beep-boop!* sound. I said hello to her in case she couldn't see who it was, and she said hello back. There was another person inside – a woman with really long brown hair. That was good. It's good to have other people floating around in a shop space when you're lifting – it keeps owners like Mrs Davies busy.

'I went over to where the bread aisle was and spied on the lady and Mrs Davies for a few seconds. Being a shoplifter is kind of like being in charge of a spaceship that's just entered a new galaxy where there's lots of planets and black holes and aliens that you have to keep your eye on in case they get dangerous. The shopkeeper is the head alien and you have to know exactly where they are at all times. That's my first big rule: never, *ever* take your eyes off the head alien.

'It all looked safe, so I picked up some of the things I was going to buy for real: bread, eggs and butter. That's my second big rule, see – to always, *always* buy something, no matter how small or cheap it is, from the shop I'm lifting things from. It makes me feel less bad, and shopkeepers never think that someone who's paying for things is also a criminal. As I bent down to pick up the things we could afford, I also picked up some things we couldn't. Like baked beans, which I slipped into my hoodie front pocket – and a small can of spaghetti that I put into my left coat pocket. Then I coughed extra loudly and slipped two packs of Mam's favourite noodles into my left coat pocket too.

'Checking that Mrs Davies was still busy, I walked over to the fridge and picked up a small bottle of milk to buy, and a pack of cheese slices to hide in my jeans pocket. They'd get squashed a bit, but Peck loves cheese on toast and he wouldn't care what it looked like.

'The door *beep-booped* again just then, and a man in a red T-shirt hurried to the counter with a large envelope in his hands. I could see the woman had joined the counter too. That was good. They'd keep Mrs Davies busy.

'I had two final things to get. Fatima's party was only four days away, and I needed to get a present for her to make her think I was normal and maybe even rich too. Mam had said, "We'll see" when I asked about going – so I wanted to be ready.

Looking totally normal, I made my way over to the birthday card rack and turned it around slowly. Most of the birthday cards in Mrs Davies' shop have been there for years – some of them look like they were printed when my grandparents were little. But I found one with balloons tied to a giraffe that looked alright enough. Checking I was in the clear, I quickly lifted my hoodie and slipped it into the waist of my jeans so that the packaging wouldn't rustle. Packets that rustle are the worst things to try and steal – you have to walk funny to stop it from rustling and attracting the head alien's attention. That's my third big rule – never take anything so noisy it might betray you. But this was for Fatima, so I had to do it.

'The door went *beep-boop!* again – the man left, and the woman with the long hair was now at the counter. She was speaking super fast, so I knew I didn't have much time for the last thing I needed to get: Fatima's present.

'I had two options. I could either get her a packet of sweets, or something from the stationery section. Both areas lay in The Black Hole Zones and were equally dangerous. Those are the areas of the shop where the eyeballs of the CCTV cameras are most likely to criss-cross with the eyeballs of humans, and suck you right up into trouble. I guess sweets and stationery are things other criminals like to take too, because in every shop I've been in, they're always right by the front counter, and have CCTV cameras pointing down at them twenty-four hours a day.

'Thinking really hard, I made a decision and headed over to the stationery section. Lots of Post-it note packets and balls of brown string and ballpens and markers that were all way too boring to give to anyone on a normal day, let alone their birthday, stared back at me. But then, on the shelf below all of them, I spotted it: the perfect gift! It was an extra-long packet of shiny animal stickers that had googly eyes on them, and a pencil with a tiger rubber on it! Fatima would definitely like them, and they went with the circus theme of her party. Maybe she would love them so much she would bring them into school, and when everyone asked where she got them from, she would say my name, and then everyone would think I was cool too!

'The door *beep-booped* again – I knew I had to be quick in case Mrs Davies got bored and wanted to spy on me. So I balanced the milk, bread, butter and eggs in one arm, and with my free hand I stuffed the stickers and pencil into the side of my jeans.

'All I had to do then was make it to the counter

without walking too funny, pay for the things I had the money for, and leave the shop still looking normal.

'Everything would still have been OK if I had followed my first rule and checked to see where everyone else was and who was orbiting Mrs Davies. But I had got so happy about finding something for Fatima that I forgot.

'Because just then, as I took my first step towards Mrs Davies and got ready to whistle and sing and make as much noise as I could to hide the noise of the crinkly packets stuffed into my trousers, a hand gripped my shoulder, pulling me back. And a voice I had never heard before thundered out across the galaxy and broke it into a million pieces with the words: "OH! MRS DAVIES! I'VE GOT A THIEF HERE!"'

# 10

## The Catch

'Have you ever had your life flash before your eyes? You know, like in the movies when people think they're about to die?' I look up at Sergeant Anita and Georgie. They both shake their heads.

'Neither have I,' I say. 'That day I think my brain tried but it couldn't come up with anything and so it made everything go black instead. Maybe you have to have done more important things than what I've done in my life for your brain to flash things at you.'

'Well now,' says Sergeant Anita, making her head go to one side. 'It seems to me that you've done lots of important things in your nine years. I don't know of many children who are caring for their mums the way you are. Or who would risk everything – even their lives – to get to London like you have today.'

'Oh yeah . . .' I say, feeling a bit happier. Maybe the next time my brain wanted to flash stuff at me, it would have more to show than just a blank, black slate.

'Did you feel scared, Audrey?' asks Georgie very gently. 'Did the hand grabbing you and the voice shouting at you make you want to run away?'

I nod – because it had been scary. Maybe one of the scariest moments of my life. Worse than when I had got caught lifting the two other times. Not because I was especially scared of Mrs Davies, but because I was scared of Mam finding out. Mam came to Mrs Davies' shop sometimes on her really, really good days.

I look up at Sergeant Anita and Georgie. 'I *was* scared,' I tell them. 'Like, really, really scared. And it just got worse . . . lots of things started going wrong all at the same time. It's like when you're setting dominoes up and accidentally knock one over, and then they all start falling over no matter how quickly you try to stop them. That's what happened after the hand gripped my shoulder and the thunder-voice made my body turn into an earthquake. I wanted to run away – but the hand was too strong and my legs jerked back, and before I knew what was happening the milk and the eggs and the bread went flying out of my arms and up into the air and then plummeted to the floor like Olympic divers. It was strange because it felt like I was watching it all in slow motion – like on the telly when they slow down a boxing match and you can see the fighters' cheeks wobbling and everything.

'Then came the noises. *THUD!* from the bread and *CRACK!* from the eggs and then the milk burst and went *GUGGLE-GUGGLE-GUGGLE!* making a flood all around my trainers.

'I think seeing the egg yolks and milk getting all mixed up together stopped my brain from being blank, because just then it told me I had to fight back. So I shouted out, "LET GO! I DIDN'T TAKE ANYTHING!" and tried to push the hand off me. But then, like they were trying to prove I was lying, the cheese slices I had squeezed into my jeans pockets jumped out and landed with a *SPLASH* in the eggs and milk. I never thought I'd get betrayed by cheese slices like that.

'Mrs Davies reached us then and asked, "What's occurring?"

'Before I could answer, the voice that ruined

everything said, "A theft's occurring, Mrs D, that's what. She's got things in her pockets – I can see them. AND I saw her put something in the back of her jeans."

'Every word made me want to run away even harder – but the hand gripping me was too strong.

'I could see Mrs Davies was upset because her face fell like broken rocks sent to crush me. "Audrey? Is that true?" she asked.

'I didn't know what to say. I wanted to tell her, "NO! I DIDN'T MEAN TO! I WAS CARRYING IT ALL TO THE TILL AND YOU'RE ALL WRONG!" But instead, hot drops of water ran out of my eyes and down my cheeks and out of my nose, and I couldn't look at anything except the blobs of white and golden-yellow on the floor that were making my trainers wet.

'"Shall we call the police?" asked the voice. Her hand was still gripping my shoulder so tightly I thought it might snap right off my body.

'I thought Mrs Davies was going to say yes, and *that* was the day you'd all come and arrest me. But instead she said, "No, I'm sure it's all just a misunderstanding."

'Just then the shop door opened again and went *beep-boop!* I didn't know who had come in, but I didn't want them to see me, so I put up my hoodie and said quietly, "I WAS going to pay for all of it, Mrs Davies! See!" I held out Mam's purse to prove my lie was true.

'Then a new voice said, "What's going on here then, Mrs Davies?"'

'Except the voice wasn't new at all. It belonged to Mo!

'The sound of it made me bow my head down lower. Mo was never going to be my friend after this. And he'd never give me another stamp. Even if he wanted to, he couldn't, because I wouldn't be able to open our front door to him or let him speak to Mam ever again – just in case he told her. My life was over.

'Mrs Davies scratched her head and said, "Oh, hello, Mo – Nessa's just caught Audrey, er . . . *hiding* a few things!"

'"Hiding! More like *taking* half the shop with her," said Nessa, who had finally let go of my shoulder.

'I turned round to look at the voice named Nessa. She had huge round eyes covered in purple glittery eyeshadow, and bright blonde hair. It looked like her head had been rubbed with balloons, because all of her hair was flying off in different directions. She looked super cool, which made her catching me feel even worse.

'"It's not true. I was going to pay for it. I promise! I did all the sums in my head and everything!" I said even louder, looking up at Mo and wanting him to believe me. Because that wasn't a lie. I was going to pay for all of it . . . just not that day. Mo was holding a stack of letters in his hand and for the first time since I had met him his face didn't have a smile on it. Instead, his eyes were large and round and worried.

'I waited for him to tell me off or shake his head. But he just said, "Mrs Davies, might we have a word outside?"

'Mrs Davies nodded, her face still droopy and sad, and with another *beep-boop!* they left the shop. They were going off to call the police – I was sure of it.

'When they left, the lady called Nessa made some tutting noises. I didn't move. I couldn't really. I just stared at the floor, wishing I could be the slices of bread that had fallen out of the packet and were now sinking into the puddle of milk and eggs.

'After about a minute, the door *beep-booped* again, and Mrs Davies' bright-blue slippers and Mo's shiny black trainers stopped in front of me.

'"Ness, you can be off now," ordered Mrs Davies.

'But Nessa didn't move. "You sure? You don't need a witness statement?" she asked.

'"Oh no, no," said Mrs Davies. "We'll get along without that. Mo and I will deal with it. Those Pot Noodles and crisps are on the house. By way of a thank-you."

'"All right, then," said Nessa after a pause. "If you're sure . . ." When she opened the door to leave, I listened for the sound of police sirens coming to get me. Swansea's small, so I knew it wouldn't take them long.

'I really expected Mo and Mrs Davies to shut the shop and put the "Closed" sign up and hold me prisoner until they came, but they didn't do either of those things. Instead, Mrs Davies told me to show her everything I had wanted to take home – and not to hide anything. So I took out the yoghurt that had stayed safe in my pocket, and the two packet of noodles and the tin of beans and spaghetti hoops and handed them to her. I think if I'd really wanted to, I could have kept Fatima's presents a secret. But I didn't want to lie to Mo and Mrs Davies. So, like a robot, I took out the stickers and the birthday card from inside my jeans and gave them to Mrs Davies too. And then I held my wrists out.

'Mrs Davies got confused and asked, "What you doing there?" I told her it was so she could put handcuffs on me, so I'd be ready to get into the police car. And then I begged Mo to tell Mam that I was sorry and that I never meant for any of it to happen.

'Mo didn't answer for a few seconds. He just looked real sad and his eyes went extra huge and watery. Then he shook his head and, covering my hands with his own, said, "We don't send one of our own off to jail for no good reason, Audrey. No one has called the police, OK? Not today."

'Then Mrs Davies said, "That's right! Now, come on then – before my regulars start coming in! Help clear up this mess, and then go and get some new bread and eggs and milk and everything your mam needs. Bring it over to me, and we'll see how much it all comes to."

'I couldn't believe my ears. Mo must have been able to tell I was too confused to move, so he took off his red Post Office bag and, placing it on the floor, grabbed a roll of tissues from Mrs Davies' counter. "Wipe your trainers with some of these, Audrey, quickly now. I can take care of the rest. *Gwneud hast!* Or your mam'll be wondering where you got to.' Then he gave me a wink like he was still my friend and began to clean up the slimy sea that had spread everywhere.

'I quickly wiped my shoes, and got a new bottle of milk, a carton of eggs, cheese slices and a fresh loaf of bread and put them all on the counter next to the birthday card and sticker set and noodles and yoghurt and cans. I knew I'd have to use my best acting skills to make Mrs Davies believe I didn't already know I couldn't afford all of it.

'When she had finished ringing up the till, Mrs Davies looked down at me over her glasses. "All together, that's seven pounds and thirty-nine pence."

'I pretended that was fine, and opened Mam's purse, and then acted really surprised to see it only had three pounds and sixty-two pence and not a ten-pound note in it like I wished it did. I told Mrs Davies that the rest of the money must be at home, and if what I had was enough for the bread and eggs – and maybe the milk – then I'd take just those and nothing else. I must have acted super well, because Mrs Davies said, "Ah, not to worry." Then she took out a large notebook from under the counter and opened it to a blank page at the back. "How about you pay for the bread and milk now, and we open an account for the rest?"

'I was well confused. I'd only ever heard of bank accounts, and Mam always said those were run by people who would sell their own grandmas. I didn't think she'd like me having one of my own just yet.

'"You mean like a bank account?" I checked.

'"No, not exactly," said Mrs Davies. "It's a different type of account. It's for when there's something you want that you don't have enough money for. All you do when that happens is you bring it to me, and I'll write the amount in my book, and you and your mam can pay me back another day, when you can. See?"

'Mrs Davies wrote out two words, and turned the book round to show me them. She'd written *Audrey's Account* in extra-pointy writing, and it made me feel all super grown-up and so happy I didn't know what to say.

'Mo had finished cleaning up and came to stand next to me. "What do you think, Audrey?"

'I wanted to tell him that I had an account book too – except I didn't know that's what it was called – and that I didn't know you could have one for things you *hadn't* stolen. But I wanted to make sure I was understanding things right, so I said, "You're saying I can take ALL these things home today? And . . . and pay you back later?"

'Mrs Davies nodded. "Not just today," she said. "Whenever you need a few things and you're short on money. You just come to the till with them, we'll put it on account, and then you can pay me back when you're ready. OK?"

'Sometimes, when someone is so nice to you – especially when you've been super naughty and don't deserve it – it feels like it can't quite be true. I've lifted lots of things from Mrs Davies *lots* of times. I know because of my own account book. So when she told me I could take whatever I needed and pay her back later, it all felt too good to be real. But then I looked at Mo and saw him nodding at me like it *was* real, and that made me feel like it might be, so I started smiling.

'Then Mo gave me a wink, and with a smile said, "Ah! But there is a catch, little miss. Well, not so much a catch really, as a bit of an opportunity . . ."'

# 11

## Bucket Lists

'An opportunity?' asks Sergeant Anita, looking interested.

'Yup,' I say. 'But it wasn't an opportunity for right then, because I had to rush home before Mam realised I was gone, and get Kat and Peck ready for school. I was so excited I felt like my heart was going to burst with all the secrets it was keeping! I wished I could tell someone all about it – about the doctor's orders and me needing to find Tad and now Mo's catch too, but then they'd find out how sick Mam really was and that I was a lifter, so I couldn't. Instead, I acted like none of those things were in my brain, and told Inara and Kavi about the two things I could tell them – first about the message in the ninja bottle and second about what I had bought for Fatima's birthday present.

Technically I *had* bought it now because of my account book with Mrs Davies, so I wasn't lying.

'Both of them said "Cool!" when they heard about the present and were so excited about the message in the bottle and the two-pound coin we had got that they wanted to start planning everything right away.

'"Let's wash the car tomorrow – straight after school," said Inara, rubbing the side of her nose happily and putting her I'm-in-charge-now voice on.

'Kavi nodded and said he didn't have rugby club the next day so he could come. I acted cool and said I was free too – as if I had lots of clubs I usually went to as well.

'"Brilliant! Let's make a bucket list then," ordered Inara.

'Kavi and me were confused about what she meant, but then Inara explained that anyone who had an old car had to have one. She knew all about it because she had an aunt who owned lots of car-wash places in Cardiff and even Port Talbot, see, and she was always talking about her bucket lists and how they got longer the older her car engines got. And since the invisible neighbour's car was so old and dusty, its list of all the things it would need to look young and shiny again would be super long.

'"I'll make the list then, yeah?" said Inara. She was well excited about it because she makes a list for everything. Before she went to Walt Disney World, she made a list that was eleven pages long – mainly to do with all the things she had to pack and what she wanted to buy and who she wanted to meet when she got there. I don't think she got to tick even half of them, but she didn't care. She says making lists makes you look forward to things more, even if they don't all come true. Especially if you use different-coloured pens for different things. So all that day, when we weren't playing foot-base, Inara wrote out our bucket list on her arm, and in last break we went over it to make sure we hadn't forgotten anything.

'At home-time, Inara and Kavi ran straight to their mams and tads. They each had to do lots of things for our car wash, and they wanted to get home straight away. I only had the one thing to do, and that was to post the note we had all written together in last break. I remember exactly what it said because we got stuck on some of the spellings. It said:

Dear X (becose you have'nt told us your name),

Thank you for the coin. We will wash your car tomorow at exaktly four after school.

Yours respektfully,
Audrey Inara and Kavi :)

'I thought it might be better to surprise whoever was there and not leave a note at all. But then Kavi said if we told them we were coming, they'd definitely stay in to see if we were washing the car properly, which would make it easier to spy back on them. Inara agreed, so before I got home I folded the note up into a mini envelope and posted it through the letterbox.'

'Did you see or hear anything that time?' asks Sergeant Anita, her pen hovering over her notebook like a spaceship about to land. 'Like the buzzing noise from before?'

I shake my head. 'There wasn't a single sound – but then I didn't stay too long 'cos Kat and Peck were with me, see. I only stayed a few seconds.'

147

Sergeant Anita nods and makes a note of something. 'And what happened next, Audrey?'

'Erm . . . well, that night, after everyone fell asleep, I stayed up late and made a new list. Except this one wasn't to do with cars. It was to do with Tad. Since the day I'd found his address, I hadn't had a single moment to sit and write the letter to him about Mam. I finally started that night. I called it my Tad Bucket List because I imagined him putting everything in a giant bucket and sending it to me. But then I guess I must have been tired, because I fell asleep halfway through and woke up late the next morning. I promised myself I'd finish it that night – right after the car wash.

'That day in school was so much fun. Inara and Kavi showed me all the things they had hidden in their rucksacks for our Bucket List. They had sponges and window-cleaning blade things and bright-coloured cloths (that looked like hair from a giant's head had been stuck on them). Inara even had pink and green spray bottles. "Extra-special window cleaners," she whispered to me, looking well proud. We had nearly everything, except Kavi had forgotten to bring his portable radio. It made Inara super annoyed because it was crucial for our plans.

'"You only had two things to get," she said. "Sponges and the radio! What are we going to do now?"

'"Well, what if we just sing extra loud?" said Kavi back. I could tell he was annoyed too because his face looked like it was on a sunbed. "I'll sing by myself if you don't want to sing without the radio. It's not like you've got the best voice on the planet!"

'"Speak for yourself," said Inara. "*Everyone* says I have the best voice. My family are always asking me to sing at Eid and things."

'"They *have* to say that," Kavi said. "They're your family," which made Inara punch him on the arm. They didn't speak to each other for the rest of the day, and I was worried that they wouldn't want to do the car wash at all after that, but then at home-time we were all so excited about our plan again I think they forgot they had even had a fight.

'After we picked up Kat and Peck, we walked as fast as we could to my street and stopped right by the car. I took Kat and Peck's school bags and ordered both of them to stay with Inara and Kavi so I could go and get the water and bucket from our house and check on Mam. She was upstairs and said she'd keep an eye on us from her window. I was super glad she wasn't downstairs – I'd told Inara and Kavi she had meetings so they couldn't come inside the house. Now, even if they tried to look in through the window or something, they wouldn't see her.

'I couldn't find a bucket, so I got two big saucepans and filled them up with warm water and enough liquid to make the bubbles extra foamy and fluffy. And then . . . have you ever washed a car with *your* best friends?' I ask, looking up at Georgie and Sergeant Anita.

'Can't say I have, I'm afraid,' Georgie says. 'I always take my car to the car wash.'

I look over at Sergeant Anita, who shakes her head no.

'You should try it,' I tell them. 'It's the most fun you'll ever have in your whole entire life! I loved it so much, I think if I wasn't going to be a doctor to help save my mam, or a world-famous stamp collector, that's what I'd want to be when I grow up – a car washer. But only if Kavi and Inara do it too. The most fun thing was splatting the windows with bubbles and then making the sponges squeak on the windows, and seeing all the dirt melt away like butter in a hot saucepan. And I'd never heard Kat and Peck giggle so much before – except for when I tickle them – and hearing them made me even happier.

'Of course, we had to complete our other mission too – which was to be so loud and annoying that it would make whoever was behind the red door come out. It was why we wanted the radio, see? To play music on it really loud and make them come out and complain, because that's what Kavi said grown-ups always do when they hear songs they're too old to know. But because we didn't have the radio, we had to think of other ways of being loud. So Inara started shouting things like, "HEY, MISTER OR MISSUS! WE'RE WASHING YOUR CAR!" and Kavi shouted, "YEAH! WE'RE GONNA MAKE IT SO SHINY YOU CAN SEE IT FROM SPACE!", and whenever Kat and Peck hugged the car to get even more soaking wet, I'd shout, "LOOK! LOOK! YOUR CAR'S GETTING CWTCHES TOO!"

'Then after a bit, Inara said, "Let's sing something!" And without waiting for us to choose a song together, she burst out into the new one by This and That – you know, the one that goes: "STRIKE BACK, BABY, BABY – UH UH YEAH! THREE STRIKES, BABY, AND YOU'RE OUT YEAH, YEAH!"

'My singing voice isn't as good as Inara's, so you'll have to imagine it better than that. Kavi joined in and did the background bits like, "YEAH, OH YEAH! OH YEAH, YEAH!" and then he started dancing – only it looked like he was being accidentally electrified.

'I started singing too – it was so much fun I couldn't help it, and soon we were all joining in with Kavi's dancing. I looked up at Mam's window in case she was watching, but I couldn't see if she was there or not. I gave her a wave anyway just in case.

'We were just getting to the second verse when Inara suddenly grabbed me and Kavi and, pointing up to one of the upstairs windows, said, "Look! Someone's there!"

'We stopped and turned to look too – but there was nothing there.

'"They were just there – I saw their glasses," said Inara. "Wave! Maybe they're still watching!"

'We all started waving right away – and Kat and Peck started shouting things like "Hello, gremp-lins" and "Whooooooo-oooooo".

152

'Then a voice said, "You're all awfully loud, dears . . . do you mind?"

'At first I thought we'd done it! That we had made the stranger come out of their house. But then Mrs Lumley's face popped up over the hedge next door and said, "I don't mind, but it upsets Maisie, it does."

'From somewhere behind the hedge, Maisie gave a loud bark and then a howl.

'We all said sorry and promised we'd be quieter.

'"Thank you," said Mrs Lumley, starting to disappear behind the hedge again. But then Inara poked me with her elbow and whispered, "*Evidence! Remember!*"

'"Oh yeah!" I whispered back. Running over to her, I cried out, "Wait, Mrs Lumley!"

'"Yes?" she asked, her face and white bun rising up again over the hedge as if she was standing on an invisible lift.

'"Mrs Lumley, I just wanted to ask you – have you heard or seen anything? From this house?" I said, pointing to the red door.

'"Yeah, like strange noises?" added Inara, who had run after me. Kavi had stayed behind to stop Peck and Kat from trying to climb both him and the car.

'"Or flashing lights?" I asked.

'Mrs Lumley frowned for a few seconds before saying, "No . . . no flashing lights. But now you come to mention it, there wasn't half a hullaballoo coming out of there last week. Sounded like drilling, it did – right next to my upstairs landing too. It unsettled my Maisie no end, so I took her out for a walk, and when we got back it was all quiet again."

'"Drilling . . ." I repeated to myself thoughtfully. What if it was *Them* – drilling special spy cameras into the walls? And of COURSE it would be upstairs! That would give them the best view of Mam's bedroom . . . I quickly looked over my shoulder to see if there were any mini camera spy balls on the outside of the house – like the ones school has near the reception wall. But I couldn't see anything. They must have all been inside.

'"Have you met who lives there yet, Mrs Lumley?" I asked out loud. "Like, in the *garden* or anything?"

'"No," said Mrs Lumley. "But their door in the back doesn't half go on being opened and closed all the time. Usually when I'm just drifting off to sleep too. Squeaks something rotten it does. No doubt someone coming in off the main road and parking up there instead of coming all the way round the front. Don't blame them, but it's always so late at night."

'Just then Maisie began barking again, so Mrs Lumley told us we were "good dears" again, and then disappeared.

'"I KNEW IT!" said Kavi, when we told him everything she said.

'"Knew what?" I asked.

'"That they're thieves! Drilling noises mean they're making an escape tunnel. Duh!"

'Kavi looked totally convinced but I knew he was wrong. A tunnel would have meant drilling noises under the ground floor, not upstairs.

'"Hold on . . ." Kavi's eyes got really big and, ignoring Kat who was hugging his leg, he said, "Do you think they let us wash the car because they needed evidence washed off? And do you think that two-pound coin was stolen?" He stared down at the sponges in his hands as if they were covered with something more than just dirty water.

'"Everyone behave normally," I whispered, even though my heart was trying to beat its way out of my chest. "They're probably still watching us. Let's dry the car, and then leave them another message. OK?"

'We finished drying and polishing the car with Inara's giant mop cloths. By the time we were done, the car was twinkling a bright-blue colour and we were all dripping wet.

'"What message shall we leave them then?" asked Kavi, looking around nervously.

'"I know," I said. Borrowing some paper from Inara's exercise book, I wrote on it:

Hello. We washd your car. We hope you like how shiney it looks. Please let us know if you like it.
Audrey, Inara and Kavi

'"You should add something mysterious," said Inara. "Like . . . 'PS. We know who you are. We heard the drilling just like what Mrs Lumley did!' You know – so they get frightened and come out of hiding to see if we really do know!"

'Kavi's mouth hung open for a few seconds before he said, "Are you *mad*? What if they really came after Audrey – or Mrs Lumley?"

'"You don't need to worry about that because I'm

*not* writing anything else," I said, rolling the message up. Now that I knew *They* were drilling secret cameras into the upstairs windows, I didn't want anything else to do with them. I just wanted to get home as fast as I could, and shut all the curtains tight forever and ever.

'Before Inara and Kavi could say anything else to me, I ran over to the red door and pushed my message through the letterbox with a super-loud clang. Not waiting to hear it drop, I ran back out on to the street and past the now sparkling car, promising myself I would keep everyone I loved as far away from the spy inside as I could. Even though they were probably looking down at me and across at Mam, right at that very moment.'

# 12

## Life Lines

'And did they?' asks Sergeant Anita, leaning back in her chair. 'Did they let you know they had seen you washing the car?'

'No – well, not then,' I say, copying her and leaning back so I can look a little bit cool like she does. 'But Mam did!'

'Really?' asks Georgie. 'And what did she say?'

'Mam said she laughed and laughed when she heard us singing – and that watching us dance made her pain disappear for a while because we had looked so funny. That made me feel super happy. Mam's laugh is one of the best sounds in the world – it's like a stream getting closer and closer and then suddenly bursting. I wish I'd been there to hear it.'

I fall quiet, wondering if, after tonight, I'll ever hear her laugh again. The chances are low, seeing as I'm thinking about her in a police station.

'After we put Kat and Peck to bed that night, I watched a film with Mam on the telly – not an old one, just a normal one. When it finished, she told me she was proud of me and gave me a cwtch. It made me feel like twenty hot-air balloons had been let go inside me, and made me even more determined to make my Tad Bucket List come true. So after I said goodnight, I waited for Mam's bedroom lamp to switch off before silently shutting my door and putting on my bedroom light.

'The plan was super simple: I had my Tad Bucket List and I had Tad's address. All I had to do was get the list to him. There's one easy way of getting a message to someone when you only have their address. And that's by the Royal Mail. I was going to write my tad a letter and ask Mo to post it for me by special services. I was sure there was a *secret* special services for post people that was faster than what normal people used, so it'd get to Tad in no time!

'That night I finished the letter I had started just the

night before, writing it out in my best handwriting so that he'd be proud of me. I had to copy it out three times because my lines kept going wonky, even though I was writing it on ruler paper I'd taken from my school diary. When I was absolutely sure it was one hundred per cent perfect, I crept downstairs to get an envelope from Mam's old business drawer in the kitchen, wrote out the address and then picked out one of my most favourite stamps. I had to find one that didn't have any ink stains or wavy lines on it so that it looked brand new. I must have looked for over an hour, but finally I found one that was perfect! It was of a mini golden kangaroo with a crown on its head. I thought my tad might like it because he used to watch a funny show with me when I was little, about a kangaroo that could box and solve mysteries.

'The next morning, when Mam wasn't looking, I asked Mo to post the letter for me extra quickly. He promised me he would and gave me a wink and tipped his cap and put it in his inside pocket to keep it safe. And I know he posted it . . . but then . . . it didn't work.'

'What do you mean, it didn't work, Audrey?' asks Sergeant Anita, frowning at me.

'The letter – it didn't get to him . . .'

Trying not to let the water in my eye sockets fall out, I reach high up my right sleeve and take out an envelope that has been folded up four times into a tight rectangle. Slowly, I place it on the table in front of me and look down at the grey sack again.

'May I?' asks Sergeant Anita, her voice all quiet and soft like a pillow.

I nod and look at the wall to the side of me. I want my eyeballs to stare at the dark-grey wall and not move, but they won't listen and swing right back to see what Sergeant Anita is doing. One of the tears I told not to fall trips out on to my cheek, so I wipe it away quickly.

Sergeant Anita carefully takes the crinkled envelope and unfolds it. On the front is my tad's address, written in my handwriting, next to a big black blob. I'd used an old envelope Mam had got from the bills people because we didn't have any new ones, but made her name and our address disappear with a black felt-tip pen. In the corner is my kangaroo stamp, next to a big Special Delivery stamp and a bar code. But both have been crossed out, and in big giant red letters inside a picture of a hand and a finger pointing to the left, are the words:

RETURN TO SENDER

'Audrey, is it OK for me to read the contents of this letter out loud?' asks Sergeant Anita. 'You can say no if you want to. But having a recording of it might help everyone understand why you did what you have done today.'

I shrug and look at the floor and whisper, 'OK.'

Clearing her throat, Sergeant Anita takes out the letter and holds it up. I can see the bright-blue ink from my favourite school pen bleeding out to the other side of the page, and the big coloured-in heart I had put in the corner, thinking it might help.

I listen as Sergeant Anita begins to read out what I wrote, thinking how different everything sounds in someone else's voice. As if they aren't my words at all but some other girl writing to some other tad. She reads:

Dear Tad,
    I hope you remembar me, even thogh

it's not Chrismas yet. Its me. Audrey. Your daughrter. I hope your well and remembar Kat and Peck too. Thank you for all your presents. We still play with them and I love all my books.

I found your adress in Mam's room, and I hope its ok, but I wanted to wriite to you becose we need your help.

    Mam is'nt well and the doctor says shes not going to get better if she does'nt get help. She needs some things that the NHS and doctor Adeola cant give her. She needs

1. A bath Room next to her bed Room – thats an on sweet.
2. A shower she can walk into.
3. A wheelchar thats elektric.
4. Hand rayls so she can walk.
5. A lift for the stayrs so she can go up and down easy.

Are they things you can get for us? I thoht becos you get us what we want for Chrismas evry year, it mihte not be hard for you to help Mam get thes things too. She never aksed you for a present, and I wo'nt this year eether if you can help. She needs them soon too befor things get too bad, or sh'ell have more and more pain and the pain killers wont be able to kill all the pain like they did befor.

I hope you can help and that you ar'nt lost any more. Even thogu London is bigger then Abertawe, and mite make you lost for a long time.

Pleese wriite back or come back and help Mam. Kat and Peck cant remembar whot you look like, and I cant remembar whot you sound like anymor. You do'nt have to stay for ever. Just a short bit to help Mam. Or if you do'nt want to come to Wales again, then maybee you can just send all the things we need.

I do'nt want Mam to get taken away or get wurse. Or us to get taken. And I no pepole are spying on us. Pleese help.

Lots of love, your daughrter,
Audrey xxxxOxxxO (the x's are kisss and the os are hugs in case you did'nt kno.)

When Sergeant Anita finishes reading, she places the letter on the table and, turning it round, pushes it back to me. It looks like a heart cut open on a surgeon's table that nobody wants.

I stare at all the lines of words written out in my best handwriting, wondering if my tad will ever see them now.

'Audrey?'

I wipe my eyes and look up at Sergeant Anita.

'Audrey, it's a very lovely letter. I can see it took you

a long time to write it, and I'm sure your dad would have really appreciated it if he'd got to read it.'

'Shall we put it away again?' asks Georgie softly.

I nod and watch as Georgie's hands, with all their shiny rings, fold up my words and runny heart and put them back again in the crumpled envelope.

We all sit in silence for a while. Sergeant Anita's eyes are all watery like two large lakes that have invisible fish swimming inside them. After a few seconds she clears her throat and speaks again.

'So . . . the letter came back to you unread?' she asks.

'Yes,' I say quietly.

'When did it come back to you?' asks Georgie, while Sergeant Anita scribbles something in her evidence book.

'The day before yesterday,' I say, sniffing.

Sergeant Anita says, 'I see, so Tuesday . . .' and then she closes her eyes and takes a deep breath. When she opens them again, all the water is gone and her eyes look normal. It's like magic.

'And what happened between then and today?' she asks. 'After the letter came back?'

'Well actually, lots of big things happened *before* the letter came back,' I say, wondering how to explain the next part of my story. 'I have to go back a bit – just a few days – to the day before Fatima's party. It was the day I started my first-ever catch job, and the night my world turned upside down all over again.'

# 13

## Stamp Duty

'What *is* this "catch" job you've mentioned, Audrey?' asks Sergeant Anita. She tilts her head to one side and leans towards me from across the table.

'Oh, it's the third best job in the world – after washing cars with your best friends and being a doctor,' I say. 'Mam thought so too.'

'Ah, so your mum knows about it?'

'Yeah. Mrs Davies asked Mo to check with Mam that she was OK with it, and she was. It just made her more proud of me, I think.'

'And what was the job?'

I sit up a little bit straighter in my chair. 'Stamp duty. Twice a week on Mondays and Fridays, for one whole hour before school. *And*! I was getting paid five pounds an hour! That means. . .' Sticking out my fingers, I quickly count out five eight times to be sure. 'Forty pounds a month!'

Sergeant Anita smiles. 'That's quite a lot of money for a girl of nine.'

'I know,' I say proudly. 'I only started the Friday just gone, but Mrs Davies is so nice that she pays me right away, so I don't have to wait for a whole month like Mam does with her payments. As soon as my hour is done, I get my five pounds. When I got my first five-pound note on Friday and then my second one just three days ago, I felt like the richest girl in Wales! I made a plan of what to do with all my money too. I was going to spend half on food and paying all the people in my little black book back bit by bit, and the other half I was going to put in a jar for anything Mam needed. I used my first wages to buy Kat and Peck their favourite crisps, and Mam a bar of her favourite chocolate. It was the best feeling ever to buy them instead of having to lift them – it made me wish I could do my stamp duty twenty-four hours a day!'

'And what does being on stamp duty entail?' asks Sergeant Anita, looking as if she wished she had the job. Her hands were making lots of notes in her evidence book too.

'It's super easy. All it is, is stamping leaflets with a special rubber stamp that has the date and the Post Office mark on it. Did you know there are thousands of leaflets the Royal Mail have to send out to every single house in the country? Some of them are dead boring – like for insurance things and travel. But then there are some really cool ones – like for brand-new stamp collections that have just come out, and for competitions too. I wanted Mam to enter some of those, but Mo said it's one of the downsides of being a Post Office or Royal Mail worker – you can't work for them *and* enter their competitions. And since I was an official actual real stamp officer, that included me now. Is that true – that I definitely can't enter the competitions?'

Sergeant Anita stops writing and looks up with a frown. 'Yes, that's true. It's also true that you're not of working age yet, and there are laws against underage labour – so *technically* Audrey, you shouldn't really be working in Mrs Davies' shop.'

I sit up straight and frown right back. 'But! But it's not labour – it's really easy! And – and I need the money . . . please don't arrest Mrs Davies! Mo and her are only trying to help me!'

'There, there, Audrey, don't get upset,' says Georgie, placing her hand on my arm. 'I'm sure Sergeant Anita can see all that.'

Sergeant Anita's frown disappears. 'Audrey, I promise Mrs Davies and Mo aren't in trouble. I'll just need to have a word with them, that's all.'

'Will that word make me lose my job?' I ask, angrily brushing a burning hot tear from my eye.

'No,' says Sergeant Anita. 'I promise. I'll just be having a word with them about getting the right permissions in place from the right people, that's all. Otherwise they could get in trouble, and we wouldn't want that, would we?'

'No,' I say, feeling instantly better. Mo and Mrs Davies will get all the permissions right away, I just know it. 'That's alright then. All the people who need to give the permissions can come and see me do my stamping if they like! I'm well good. On my first day on the job I was so quick that Mrs Davies said I was the fastest stamper she had ever seen. And she let me sit next to her, right behind the counter where all the books of stamps and special signs are. I start my job at six thirty in the morning – so I get to see all the things Mrs Davies does before she opens the shop at seven, and I get home by seven thirty-five, which means I can still get Kat and Peck and myself ready for school. Mam started waking up early on the days I had to work too – so she could make sure I got up on time and looked smart. I knew she wished she could come and see me do the stamping too, so I told her that when she was feeling stronger, and the weather was a bit warmer, I'd pay for a taxi with my new money so she could see me in action.

'I told Inara and Kavi I was a Royal Mail stamper right away on Friday. Inara's eyes popped out like slices of toast jumping out of a toaster, and when Kavi heard, he cried out "Whoa-Whoa WHOA!" at least five times and gave me half a roll of his fruit pastilles as a congratulations present. They asked me if I had to wear a suit and how many leaflets I could stamp in a minute and how much I was getting paid. I told them it wasn't much – just a few pounds and that it was no big deal. But really, I think they knew it was the biggest deal on the planet! Nobody else in my year had a job yet – at least, not one that wasn't just for pocket money from their mams and tads. I was the first one! I didn't even care if anyone in school saw me. Having a job was a billion times better than me being a lifter – and *They* couldn't take Mam away when I was earning proper real money.

'Those two moments last week – Thursday when I asked Mo to post my letter for Tad, and that Friday morning when I started my new duties – were some of the best moments of my whole entire life. From the second I posted the letter and while I did my Stamp Duty, I kept imagining my letter getting to Tad, and him buying whole new bathrooms and electric wheelchairs, and planning how he was going to surprise us with them soon.

'All that Friday, everything at school felt more exciting than usual. After I told Inara and Kavi about my new job, they went and told all our other friends, who said they wanted to go on stamp duty too! I'd never done anything that everyone else wanted to do before – it was usually the other way around, and it made me feel like it was secretly my birthday. I got the same tingling feeling I did when I brought the SHOUT!

bar into school that time. The other thing everyone was talking about all day was Fatima's party. With just one day to go, the stories about what was going to happen had got wild. There were rumours that Mr Garcia had bought her a robot dog, and that flying acrobats were going to be swinging their way across Wales to be there. Oliver said he'd heard there was a one hundred million per cent chance a man was going to be shot out of a cannon.

'I didn't believe any of the rumours except maybe the flying acrobats one, but Inara and Kavi believed them all. The truth was, I didn't care if not even one was true. If all we did was sing Fatima the happy birthday song and eat cake, I'd still be the happiest I'd ever been, because it would be my first ever birthday-party experience. Mam had told me I could go to the party the night before, see – just for two hours. She had asked Mo if he could take me and bring me back again. She said she would be fine as long as Kat and Peck didn't get too naughty, and that she wanted me to store as many photos in my head so that I could come home and tell her all about it. Mam was going to let me put some of her glitter on my eyes – and she'd said I could borrow a hat with coloured feathers my grandma had left behind and pretend to be a human parrot. I'd even practised my "Ka-Kaaaaa" noises.

'By that Friday afternoon, no one could be bothered to do lessons properly. We were way too excited – even the teachers had given up. Mrs Li usually makes us do a test every Friday to see if we've been listening all week. But that day she wheeled a great big TV into the class and let us watch a whole hour of *Puff the Magic Dragon* instead. It was like the party had already started.

'I was so happy on the way home from school, I bought Kat and Peck those crisps I told you about before and Mam's bar of chocolate from Mrs Davies' shop. Using my first five-pound note to pay for it made me feel ten feet tall. And as soon as we got in, I cried out, "Mam! We're home!" She wasn't downstairs, so Kat and Peck ran upstairs to find her.

'I was just getting the bread out to make tea, when suddenly I heard a scream.

'Hearing that scream made everything inside me crack like I was a vase that'd had a brick thrown at it.

'I dropped the bread on the floor and ran up the

stairs as fast as my legs would go. Kat and Peck were both standing in Mam's room, looking scared with their hands in their mouths and their eyes and faces wet with tears. And – and Mam was on the floor . . . looking like a doll that had accidentally been dropped.

'Rushing over to her, I fell on to my knees. I shouted "MAM!" at her and gave her shoulders a shake. But she didn't move and her eyes were closed. I pressed my ear to her chest.

'*Ba-boom. Ba-boom.*

'She was alive. She was still ours.

'For a split second, the loud stamping in my heart made my hands go numb and my mind go blank. But then they sprang back to life and I grabbed the phone to dial 999. And before whoever was on the other end of the line could say a single word, I finally let out a scream and heard my own voice, crying out for help.'

# 14

## Snail Mail

'That must have been very scary, Audrey,' says Georgie, leaning closer to me.

I stare down at the sack in my hand and begin twisting a corner of it round and round and round, until it won't twist any more.

Sergeant Anita moves forward in her chair. 'Audrey, I understand this is an incredibly difficult moment to speak about. Would you like a break? Georgie can take you outside if you like, so you can get some fresh air?'

Letting the corner of the sack go, I watch it twirl like a spinning ballerina until it becomes itself again. I know that once I leave this room I won't want to come back to it again. The grey walls feel like they're secretly tiptoeing closer and closer, so that they can hear me too.

'No – I – I want to finish in one go and then go home,' I say, taking a sip of what's left of my squash. Sitting up straight, I look over at the round black watch on Sergeant Anita's wrist, and watch as the tall hand jumps forward as if it's leaping over the world's tiniest lake.

'So, Audrey, after you found your mum on the floor like that, you called the emergency services. Did that – incident make you decide to do what you did today?'

I nod silently, keeping my eyes fixed on her watch and telling myself not to blink so that I don't see the image of Mam on the floor again behind my eyelids. I never, ever, ever want to see it again . . . Mam's arms sprawled away from her and bent like they were broken . . . her legs looking all twisted. The last two times I had found Mam, she hadn't been on the floor like that. The very first time she'd been downstairs in the bathroom. And she had been in her chair the second time – up in her room. Both times weren't as scary as Friday.

'Did the ambulance take her away?' asks Sergeant Anita more softly.

I shake my head. 'No . . . they didn't need to. Dr

Wilson – that was one of the ambulance doctors, he said Mam hadn't taken her medicine on time, that's all. It only took them a few minutes to wake her up again. And when she came back, she said she'd felt dizzy, and realised she'd forgotten to bring her medicine bag with her from the living room. Then all she remembered was walking to the bedroom door to go down and everything went black.

Dr Cassie – that's the other ambulance doctor, she said it happened all the time, and that I wasn't to worry and that I had done the right thing by calling them immediately. She also said Mam hadn't eaten enough so her sugar levels had dropped, which wasn't good, especially for someone who needed a lot of medicines. So we were to make sure she always had a full tummy.

'Mam kept shaking her head and saying, "I can't believe I've been so silly" and "It won't happen again." Every time she said that, I made a silent promise: *I'd* make *sure* it wouldn't. Not *ever*. After one of the other times Mam had fallen and I'd thought my life was over, I'd asked Dr Adeola for two canes for her instead of just one, so I could make sure she never lost her balance again. And now that I had a job and an account, I could make sure Mam never went hungry again either. I decided I'd ask Mrs Davies if I could work every day the next time I saw her – even Sundays, and if she knew any other shops that needed a stamper, so that I could make lots more money and I'd always have enough, no matter what.

'Kat and Peck were so scared they stayed quiet almost the whole time the ambulance doctors were in our house. They didn't say anything even when Dr Wilson and Dr Cassie winked at them and told them Mam was going to be fine. They just stood close to me and stared at everything. I could feel their fingers clinging on to my legs.

'Dr Cassie told Mam it would be good for her to go into hospital and stay the night so that people could watch her, and asked if there was anywhere we could go if she did that. But Mam shook her head. We both knew how much she hated hospitals. Her worst nightmare is being stuck in one for the rest of her life.

'"I'm feeling a million times better," she said. The doctors had given her some juice, so she held it up and said it was already making all the difference in the world.

'I'm not sure Dr Cassie believed her because she went, "Hmmmmm," and placed the big black blood-pressure cuff around Mam's arm again. We all waited as the noise of it getting tighter and tighter and then suddenly letting go of all its air filled the room. Then they checked Mam's heartbeat again with the stethoscope, and finally Dr Cassie looked over her shoulder at Dr Wilson and gave a nod. "All sound. Think we're good here."

'When they'd packed up all their things, Mam said, "Thank you both so much," and leaned forward in her chair. I could tell by her eyes that she wished she could get up and shake their hands and walk them downstairs to the door like she would have done if her body hadn't got in the way.

'"Yeah, thank you," I said, doing it for her instead. I held out my hand to Dr Cassie and then to Dr Wilson and shook theirs extra hard for both Mam and me. Peck and Kat wanted to shake their hands too, so I let them. Now that they could see Mam was OK, they were coming back to being themselves again – like statues that had come back to life after a spell had been broken. Kat even asked if she could have a go on the walkie-talkie.

'When they got to the front door, the doctors both said "Bye!" and "*Cymerwch ofal nawr!*" and shook my hand again. I wanted to hug them both tight and say, "*Diolch, diolch, diolch*" a million times – but that wouldn't be professional or grown-up. Instead, I stood up real straight and watched them walk to the ambulance. They looked like real-life superheroes. I'd forgotten the ambulance was there, with its lights flashing blue and red and white and silver and orange all at once. And I suddenly noticed that nearly the whole street had come out to see what was going on. That's the problem with ambulances – and police cars: everyone always knows when there's one nearby. And everyone always wants to know why it's arrived and who it's come to help.

'I spotted Mrs Lumley with her dog, peeking out from behind her bushes, and Mr Ghosh to the right of us, pretending to water flowers that were already dripping wet – and even Mr Jahangir and his wife standing at their front gate, holding their baby and looking like they'd never been outside before. Every front garden had someone in it, it seemed – except for the house opposite. I stared up at it and saw something glimmer from the top window. But it was gone in a second – and I couldn't tell if it was something shining from inside or just a reflection of the ambulance lights.

'After the ambulance and its lights and the super doctors had left, I hurried Kat and Peck inside and shut the door on everyone as quickly as I could. But, it turned out, my downward rollercoaster ride bit of the day hadn't finished yet. Because later that night I saw it again. A glimmer of bright white light – from the house opposite. It happened at exactly ten seventeen p.m. – I know because I wrote the time and all the details in my Welsh Inquisition Book the next day.

'I'd been sitting with Mam in her room, watching one of our favourite cartoon films together. Kat and Peck had fallen asleep on Mam's bed because they didn't want to leave her that night either, and Mam had started dozing off too, when suddenly I noticed a flash on the telly – a silver light. It was being reflected from the window. I carefully got up off the arm bit of Mam's armchair and ran over to the window – where it happened again! Two white lights flashing from the window directly opposite ours. Then everything went dark again. Just like before. I knew it was *Them*. It had to be! Those flashes were just like the flashes of a camera or a phone, taking pictures in the dark – they had obviously seen the ambulance and knew Mam wasn't well and were now trying to get pictures of her being too sick to look after us!

'Mam hated having the curtains closed – she said she felt closet-phobic if she couldn't see the outside world. But that night I closed them super tight, and went and got a big towel from the bathroom and hung that over the curtain rail too. Mam was well confused when she woke up and saw it there, so I lied and said I could feel the cold coming in and didn't want her or Kat and Peck to catch anything.

'I wished the next day had been a school day and not the weekend, because I wanted to tell Inara and Kavi about the spies right away. But of course, the next day was Saturday – the day of Fatima's party. Mam seemed a bit better that morning – but her skin still looked like it had a ghost trapped underneath it, so I made her all her favourite things for breakfast and reminded her that I had a job now so she shouldn't ever not eat again. I also told her that I wouldn't be leaving her side for even one second the whole weekend, even if it really annoyed her. Even though that meant . . .'

The hard-boiled egg that always lives in my chest suddenly bobs up into my throat and stops all my words.

'Even though that meant . . . you wouldn't be able to go to Fatima's party?' finishes Georgie for me.

I push the egg down hard and tell it to go away. It scrapes its way down my throat like a car going down an alleyway that's too small for it and lands back in my chest.

'I didn't care,' I say, acting like I really hadn't, and shrugging. 'Mam's more important than any party. And then – well, Mo knocked on our door and made me forget about it. Not that he meant to.

'I'd just got Mam her breakfast when he knocked his usual three knocks. After saying "Good morning, little madam, how are you doing today?" like normal, he asked me how Mam was because it seemed that everyone in Swansea knew an ambulance had come to see her. He wanted me to pass his and Mrs Davies' regards on to her. I'm not sure why grown-ups like passing on regards instead of chocolates, but I said I would.

'"So – am I still picking you up to take you to your friend's party later?" he asked. From the sad look in his eyes, I could tell he knew the answer already.

'I shook my head. "I – I want to stay with Mam. She's totally fine – but I just want to."

'Mo bobbed his head up and down for a few seconds, and then said, "Well . . . good thing I've got an extra-special delivery for you then."

'He held out his hand all curled up into a tight stone and waited. It was a stamp! He hadn't brought me one in days, and whenever he gave me a stamp that way I knew it was going to be a super-special one. I tapped his hand, just like I always did, and watched his fingers open up like a flower to reveal the stamp in the middle of his palm. It had the picture of an island with palm trees on it, and bright-blue water, and a teeny-tiny whale spouting water in the right-hand corner. I had never seen it before and felt my insides roar and cheer and wish it could come to life, so that I could go for a swim in it.

'"It's from the DR," he said, pointing to the words "REPUBLICA DOMINICANA" written in tiny green print on the left-hand corner. At the top was a quarter of a circle and three faint wavy black lines, which meant Mo had peeled it off an envelope.

'I didn't know where that was and wished I had a map to find it. But then Mo explained it's an island just off the coast of America and Mexico and that it was where he was born.

'"Really?" I asked, surprised. "I thought you were Welsh!"

'That made him smile and say, "I'm that too. You can come from more than one place and belong to both of them. That's the magic of our world."

'I promised Mo I'd take extra-special care of the stamp and asked him what it was like in the DR.

'He said there were palm trees and coconut trees and banana trees and sandy crescent beaches as far as the eye can see. And in the oceans all around it, there are baby whales with their mums singing. Then he said, "Maybe one day you can go and see it for yourself."

'I said, "Maybe," even though I know I'll never get to. I've never been outside of Wales, let alone a whole other country. Well, not until today, that is.

'After he gave me the stamp, I asked him if he had

posted Tad's letter and if he thought it might have reached Tad's house already. Mo nodded and said, "Absolutely, little miss! I made it a priority of mine. It was sent Special Delivery too – so it should be with him about now. Depends on if he's got a postman as good as me!" He chuckled for a few seconds and then asked, "Is there a reason you're trying to get in touch with your tad then?"

'I didn't reply straight away, because I was wondering if I should tell him about the doctor's orders and the flashing lights and *Them* getting evidence together in all their evidence books to take Mam away from us. But before I could decide, Mrs Lumley from across the street came back from her morning walk with Maisie and shouted "*Bore da Mo!*", and took the moment away. Mo tipped his cap at me and, giving me a wink, went off to go and talk to her instead.

'All that weekend I looked after Mam super carefully and tried to keep her away from the windows. And all that weekend I focused on not thinking about the party and how much fun everyone was having without me and how big the birthday cake had been. Instead, I tried to think about what Tad might be doing with my letter. That was what really mattered – Tad's letter and him getting it.

'By Monday morning, Mam still wasn't a hundred per cent better. She wasn't having a Nightmare Day, but she was still sore and in pain. Even though it seemed like the worst might be over, and the sick feeling right at the bottom of my tummy was starting to go, I knew I couldn't leave her – not to go to school anyway. I did leave her to go to Mrs Davies' and get my second five-pound note, but only because she was sleeping. After I got back and she was up, I dropped off Kat and Peck at our normal place and then ran right back home to look after her.

'Dr Adeola stopped by in his lunch break to make sure she was OK, and even though Mam didn't want me to, I heard her crying again and begging him to speed up the applications he'd talked about, because she couldn't go on for much longer like this. Hearing her say those words made my chest feel like it was getting squeezed so hard I couldn't breathe. I wished harder for Tad's gifts to get to us soon.

'But then Tuesday came. And . . . I knew something was wrong when I opened the door and Mo wasn't smiling as usual. It was like the sun had been covered by a big grey cloud.

'He said, "Morning, little miss. I, er . . . I'm afraid I have a delivery for you . . ." and held it out to me – the envelope I had written for Tad, all covered in crosses and the marks and red words. Like a piece of art that had been vandalised.

'I stayed quiet, but I think Mo could tell I was upset because he kept saying things. First he said, "It looks like your tad might have moved from that address, little miss." When I didn't say anything, he added, "Or maybe they didn't recognise who 'Tad' was – you could try writing back and putting your tad's full name on it?" When I still didn't say anything, he said, "If he has moved, the person living there might know where he's moved to. You can write back and ask them that too." After another long silence he finally said, "Ah, I'm sorry, Audrey – sometimes snail mail just doesn't do the job we need."

'I still didn't say anything back. I couldn't, because I knew as soon as I opened my mouth I would start to cry. So I took the letter and, with a nod and a silent wave to Mo, went and hid it with my stamps.

'Mam told me I had to go back to school that day because she was much better, so in the playground, while Kavi and Inara told me all about the party and how there weren't any acrobats but there was a man in a top hat and a donkey dressed like a unicorn, I thought about what Mo had said about snail mail, and how much time I'd wasted thinking Tad had read my letter when really, it had just been making its way back to me. I lied to Kavi and Inara and everyone else at school who had heard about the ambulance coming to my house, and said it had come to see me because I'd twisted my ankle. I don't think I even told Kavi and Inara about the flashing lights – not that day anyway. I had too much to think about.

'That night, when the house was quiet and Mam and Kat and Peck were all sleeping, I crept back to my room and took out my stamps box and Tad's letter. What if the person at Tad's address *did* know where he was and all I needed to do was ask them – just like Mo said? Or! What if Tad *was* there, but he couldn't read my handwriting properly? Mrs Li was always telling me my a's needed to look less like o's – so maybe he thought "Tad" had been "Tod", and because it was illegal to open someone else's letters, he had sent it back, not knowing it was from me! Not knowing how badly we needed his help, or how close *They* were!

'I don't know how long I sat there thinking, but after a while, my fingers found a stamp with a picture of a cheetah on it, and an idea started knocking on all the doors inside my brain. If I was the fastest-running animal in the whole world, I'd speed my way to Tad's address and knock on his door and see who was there. And if it was him, then I could ask him for help in person. And if it was someone else living there, I'd ask them where he'd moved to and then sprint right there too! And I'd do it so quickly, no one would even know I was gone . . .

'And then suddenly, I knew what I could do! There *was* a way I could reach Tad's address so fast that no one would see me, let alone catch me – just like a cheetah running at full speed. All I needed was a little help from Inara and Kavi, and, without her knowing it, Mrs Davies too . . .'

# 15

## Super Secret Special Forces

'I – I know it's wrong to ask your friends to do something that might get them into trouble. But Inara and Kavi only did it because I asked them to – you won't tell their mams and tads, will you? And – and Mrs Davies didn't even know at all, so it wasn't her fault. It was all me – no one else, OK? Cross my heart and hope not to die.'

I look up at Sergeant Anita and Georgie, and wait for them to promise that Kavi and Inara won't get into trouble.

'We're not looking to punish anyone at all,' says Sergeant Anita.

Georgie adds, 'Audrey, all Sergeant Anita wants to do is help everyone at the Royal Mail figure out exactly what happened. How you were able to travel as far as you did, the way you did. It was so very dangerous, and they just want to make sure they can stop anyone else trying the same thing. That's all.'

'Exactly,' says Sergeant Anita. 'You were lucky to have escaped today without being seriously hurt – or worse. My job is to help protect people – to safeguard everyone. So I have to try and understand how you managed to get here, and make sure it never happens again. It's not about punishing you, or anyone else, at all, OK?'

Looking down at the tears in the legs of my dungarees, and the plasters covering the scratches on my knees, I nod. I did get hurt lots of times today, and I guess I was quite lucky none of my bones got broken.

'So, let's go back a moment. When exactly did you tell Kavi and Inara about your plan and ask them to help you?' asks Sergeant Anita, drawing a line under some words in her evidence book.

'I told them yesterday – in the lunch queue.'

Georgie splutters and coughs, before saying in a shocked voice, 'You put this plan together in your lunch break?'

'And a bit of last break too,' I add, since she seems

surprised. 'But even before I told them anything, I did my research. When Mo knocked yesterday morning like usual, I asked him all the questions I needed to know. Like, how long it would take for super-extra-special mail to get from Swansea to London, and what the names of all the different types of express deliveries were. He started listing them but there were so many, I can't remember all of them without my Welsh Inquisition Book. He seemed a bit suspicious at first of all the questions, but I told him it was part of my investigation – the one he'd already helped me with when I needed to find out about the neighbours. I guess me acting like a reporter and a detective worked because he answered everything.

'Then, on the way to school, I stopped at Mrs Davies' and asked questions about what different types of delivery vans the Royal Mail had, and which one was the fastest, and how much it cost to send really heavy things. I told her it was for a class project.

'If you had special permissions and had kids working for the police, I bet you could get *all* the criminals to talk. Everyone tells you everything when they think it's for a class project.'

I look up at Sergeant Anita, who gives me a small smile. I think she's as impressed with my idea as I am.

'By the time I got to school and had dropped off Kat and Peck to their bit of the playground, my plan was all good and ready. It was like a map had opened up in my head and I knew exactly where I had to go now. I couldn't wait to tell Kavi and Inara about it right away – except I couldn't, because they and everyone else still wanted to talk about Fatima's party. I couldn't get Inara and Kavi alone even for a second before school started or at first break or at lunch break – it felt like half the school were all joined together in one big scrum made of whispers.

'It was only when we got to the line for school dinners that finally we weren't surrounded by everyone else. So right between the veggie fingers and chips queue, I started telling them, and by the time we reached the pudding dinner lady they'd heard my whole plan. It wasn't a long one, so it didn't take much time to explain.

'Inara was the first one to understand it because she shouted out, "Wait. You want to do WHAT?"

'Then a few seconds later Kavi must have understood it too, because he said, "Yeah . . . you want to do

WHAT?" He was staring at me with his mouth so wide open, I could see all the fruit pastilles he'd been chewing.

'I told them to shush – Nutan and Larry and everyone were staring at us. I hurried them to our usual table in the corner of the dinner hall and, before anyone else could join us, repeated my plan. Then they both asked me why. I'd forgotten they might ask me that and that they didn't know about my letter to Tad. I didn't have an answer ready, so I started to tell them that there was a super-important thing in London that Mam urgently needed for her job and that I wanted to surprise her with . . . but then something weird happened. My mouth started making the words come out slower and slower, until they all stopped, and I couldn't tell the lie any more. I think maybe you can only act for so long before your body stops you, and that's why really famous actors disappear after a while – they just get too tired to pretend any more. I think that's what happened to me. So I told them the truth – but only the short version. I told them that I needed Tad to help us right away, because Mam was ill.

'When I finished saying those last three words to Inara and Kavi, I felt my throat starting to choke me.

I think that was the first time I'd ever said them out loud in front of anyone who wasn't a doctor. And suddenly it made me worried that I had said too much – I didn't want Inara and Kavi to look at me different or feel sorry for me or Mam.

'I could tell they both wanted to say something, but just then Larry and Angie and Nutan came and joined our table, and all of them started going on about Fatima's party again – this time about the goodie bags. I stayed silent and gobbled up my lunch extra quick. Inara and Kavi did the same, and as soon as we could we all ran out into the playground together.

'"So – so will you help me?" I asked, before they could say anything about Mam.

'Kavi looked over at Inara, and Inara looked over at him, and then they looked at me and stared again.

'"Well, will you?" I asked louder, feeling desperate. The plan wouldn't work without them. I needed them to say yes! "Please?"

'Inara gave a nod. "Yeah. It's for your mam. We know she's not been well for ages."

'"You do?" I asked.

'"Yeah," she said. And then she added, "Our mams

are still friends, remember? My mam messages your mam sometimes to see how she is. Especially, you know, when I tell her you're not in school again."

'"She does?" I nearly shouted.

'"Mine too," said Kavi. "My parents have been friends with your mam since we became friends, remember?"

'"I forgot," I said honestly, wondering why they had both never said anything to me before – especially when I talked about Mam working all the time.

'"She – she must be really sick if you need to find your tad," said Inara really quietly. "Isn't there any other way you can get to him – that isn't, you know, so dangerous?"

'Shaking my head, I took out Tad's letter from my school trouser pocket. "I've tried. But Mo said maybe Tad didn't open the letter because I didn't put his whole name on it – or he might have moved. And the only way I can find out where he's moved to is by going there and asking the new people there if they have his new address. I – I don't have time to try another letter. I can't wait any longer. Especially after what happened this weekend."

'"You mean with the ambulance – and your ankle?"' asked Kavi, taking a step towards me with his eyes jumping out.

'"Yeah," I said. "Only, the ambulance wasn't for me. It was for Mam." I watched Inara's and Kavi's faces stare at me, as the true words came flooding out of me. "Mam fell down – really badly – and the ambulance doctors had to come and wake her up again. But the medicines she takes aren't enough any more. I've got to get lots of things for her to make her better again but they're all super-expensive things – like an electric wheelchair and a bathroom and even a lift for the stairs. And even though I've got my stamping job now, it won't be enough. That's why I have to go and ask Tad – tomorrow. Before things get worse and Mam hurts herself again. Or the spies across the road get us."

'"Wait, I thought the people across the road were robbers!" said Kavi.

'"I'm pretty sure they're spies," I said, deciding to tell them everything. "Spies that I think are trying to take Mam away from us."

'"NO!" cried out Inara, gasping. "Why would anyone take your mam away from you?"

200

'I told them all about the documentary I'd watched about social teams inspecting families and taking children away from mams and tads who couldn't look after their kids properly, and about the flashing lights too. Inara and Kavi listened silently. When I was done, I waited for them to say something. And while I waited, even though we were standing in what was probably the loudest playground in Wales, I couldn't hear anything except my heartbeats.

'Finally Inara grabbed my arm and said, "OK. I'm in. We can't let your mam get taken away from you."

'"Yeah," said Kavi. "But we better not get caught or we'll end up in jail and my tad will kill me."

'"We won't get caught," I promised. "My plan is going to definitely work."

'"But Post Offices don't open before nine, do they?" asked Kavi. "What are we going to do about school? We can't *all* not show up!"

'"Mrs Davies' shop opens at seven,' I said. "She's a real postmistress and everything. And this morning she told me everything about all the different parcels and what happens to them. I've got it all down in my inquisition book. All we have to do is get same-day, super-special, super-fast delivery. That's the one where the Post Office and Royal Mail and all their forces HAVE to get your post delivered that exact same day – by exactly one o'clock, because it's the post law."

'"Whoa," said Inara. I could tell she was getting excited then because she was starting to rub her nose more, and faster too – like it was a lamp and she was trying to get a genie to come out. "That's like magic, that is."

'"I know," I said, getting excited too. "And Mo said there's all kinds of special force vans and trucks across the country who help the post get to where it's supposed to go on time. We could do it in a day and no one would ever know. All you have to do is help me get to Mrs Davies', drop off Kat and Peck, and cover for me when I'm mitching. I'll be back before you know it!"'

'Sorry Audrey – what does "mitching" mean?' asks Georgie, half-whispering.

'Oh – you know – when you're not in school even though you're meant to be,' I explain.

'Ah! *Bunking*,' says Georgie. 'I understand. Please continue.'

Wondering what bunkbeds had to do with mitching,

I go back to explaining what happened. 'And then Kavi said, "But what about the money? I bet getting special trucks and things is super expensive. I've only got, like, sixty-three pence saved up.'

'"Don't worry," I said, apologising to Mam in my head already. "I'll get the money. Just come to my house before school tomorrow. I'll take care of everything else. Remember, this is top secret – so we can't say a word to anyone."

'We all nodded at each other – like we were a special post force too – except without a van. But then Inara grabbed my arm and shook it really hard and said, "Hold on! How exactly are we *getting* to Mrs Davies'? *It* will be too heavy for me and Kavi to carry on our own."

'We all fell quiet. Inara was right – there was no way my idea would work if we couldn't even get to the Post Office to begin with. I hadn't thought of that! The map began to crumple up like a piece of paper in front of my eyes. But then Inara cried out, "Got it," and slapped Kavi on the arm. And, grinning so widely that she looked like that strange cat in *Alice in Wonderland*, she whispered the word "Scooters!"'

# 16

## Signed, Sealed, Delivered . . .

'Ah, so THAT's how Kavi and Inara transported you,' says Sergeant Anita. 'With scooters!'

Georgie covers her mouth and gives a short laugh. I think I even hear her say the word 'Genius!'

'Yeah. But if Mam hadn't said about the old washing-machine box last night, Kavi and Inara wouldn't have had anything to carry me in, and today might not have happened at all. I was really lucky she remembered it. I had to lie and tell her it was for school again. It wasn't a big red lie, but it wasn't a small white one either, so I guess it was like a pinkish lie. I told her that I needed to find the biggest cardboard box I could find for a project about homeless people. She said the old washing machine box was still in the shed and would that do?

'When she said that, I felt like that football stadium inside me that roars when it sees a new stamp come to life. It wasn't quite as loud as that, but it came close! I hurried to the shed with Kat and Peck following me and pushed lots of things out of the way to find it. It was covered in dust but it was still strong, and had some of Tad's things stuffed inside it – like his old trainers and a bicycle pump and some magazines – most of them about rugby. Mam ordered me to put them all in the bin when I showed them to her, but I thought he might like them back – especially if he came to help Mam maybe, and see Kat and Peck, and me too. So I secretly put them in some bags and hid them back in the shed.

'Then I spent the whole evening polishing the outside of the box and making the inside all clean and cosy too. I told Mam I had to fill it with things that someone without a house might need to stay all warm and safe in, and she said I could borrow the nearly-flat cushions from the sofa, and Kat and Peck's fuzzy blue blanket with the paws on it, and her woolly gloves too – the ones that stop her bones from freezing and the pain getting worse when it's autumn and winter. I promised her I'd be careful and bring it all back, and now . . . now she's going to be so mad when she finds out I've lost all of it. I should never have taken her gloves. You – you couldn't ask the Royal Mail people to give them back to me, could you? You know, if they find them?'

I look up at Georgie, but she just smiles and passes my look on to Sergeant Anita.

'Only, Mam's had those gloves forever. I think my mam-gu – that's my mam's mam – knitted them for her. Oh! And my stamps too!' I add. 'I stuck all my most favourite stamps on the box last night after everyone went to sleep – for luck. They were all the special ones Mo gave me – even his Dominican Republic one. I think there were sixty-two of them. Could you please, please ask the Royal Mail people to give the box back to me – even if it's all smashed up now, so I can get them back? They're my private collection and can't ever be replaced. Kind of like Mam's gloves. And our sofa cushions too, probably. Oh – and Kavi's cap – the scrum one! It's bright red with a white dragon on the front, and it looks like there's ice cubes inside it.'

Sergeant Anita's hand and pen are moving faster and faster and making lots of notes, when suddenly they both stop. 'Scrum cap?' she asks.

'It's a special hat for rugby – Kavi wears it because his mam's afraid his brain will get all shaken up like milkshake in the games. After him and Inara got to my house this morning, he gave it to me to wear. He said his sister's parcels were always arriving all broken and looking like they'd been kicked around, so I had to wear it for protection. It was super nice of him – he's never let me or anyone else at school try it before, not even just for fun, and when I put it on it made me feel like Amelia Earhart must have done when she first got into her plane – all brave and cool! We read about her last year. She's like a parcel that got lost in the post and hasn't been found yet. I kind of wished I had goggles like hers – you know, the ones pilots wear. But having Kavi's cap was cool enough.'

'What time did Inara and Kavi get to your house this morning, Audrey? Do you remember?' asks Sergeant Anita.

'Yup. It was exactly eight twenty-two – I know because Mam was still downstairs at eight, and I was worried she wouldn't go back up before they were supposed to arrive. She'd come downstairs to use the bathroom, and had stayed to say hi to Mo when he came. I acted like everything was normal while they talked, but inside I was so nervous I think I even went deaf for a bit. Because what was I going to do if they were both still there when Inara and Kavi came? But I got lucky, because at exactly eight twenty Mo tipped his cap at Mam and left, and she headed back upstairs slowly. Kat and Peck were eating their cereal and watching *Ivor the Engine* in her room, and wanted her to watch it with them. The second she disappeared at the top of the stairs, I ran to the front window to watch for Inara and Kavi. It was exactly eight twenty-one then, but they weren't there like they were supposed to be. So I was staring out at my street, when suddenly the door to number forty-two – it opened!'

'No!' says Georgie, sitting up straight.

'It did – but just then Inara and Kavi appeared round the corner with their scooters and the door quickly shut again! I opened my door before Inara or Kavi could knock, and pulled them inside.

'"Sssssssh! Quick," I told them. "The red door over

there just opened! I think someone was going to come out but didn't because they saw you!"

'"No WAY!" whispered Inara. "Let's look!"

'We all ran to the window and watched for a few seconds, but the door didn't open again.

'"Come on – we better leave it and go," I said after a moment. "Kat and Peck's cartoon's going to end soon." I took them over to the kitchen where the box was, and noticed them both looking around my house like it was secretly a museum.

'"Your house is well nice," said Inara.

'"Thanks," I said, feeling pleased. I'd tidied everything up last night and hidden all of Kat's and Peck's toys behind the sofa.

'"Hold the mobile phone! Is this the box?" asked Kavi so loudly that Inara had to thump him to shush him. "It's well tidy!" he whispered. "You'll be comfy in there. I like all these stamps too. Where did you get them from?"

'"Just from letters and things," I whispered back. I still didn't want him or Inara to know I was a stamp collector. I'd already told them so many of my Top Secrets, and this one I still wanted to keep.

'"Cool," said Kavi quietly. "The cushions are good . . . but here, have this too. For extra protection." That's when he pulled out his scrum cap. Then Inara gave me her blackcurrant squash drink and lunch box too, so that I wouldn't get hungry. I hadn't even thought about anything like that. I wanted to say thank you, but didn't know how, so I gave them both grins instead.

'That was when Mam called out for me. The cartoon had finished and it was time for Kat and Peck and me to go to school. This was it! Go-time – and no matter what, I had to make sure Mam didn't come down the stairs before the box and us had all left the house.

'So I shouted back "I'M COMING!" really loudly, and signalled to Kavi and Inara to get in a huddle. "Remember the plan," I said, really quickly. "And don't forget," I added, pointing to the piece of paper on the kitchen counter, sitting under a pair of scissors and some tape. I'd written out Tad's full name and address in giant black letters so that no one could deliver me to the wrong place.

'"Got it," whispered Inara.

'"And here's the money," I said, handing her a tissue with three notes wrapped up inside it. After Inara and

Kavi said they'd help me, I'd gone to the cash machine on the way home from school and taken out everything except for ten pounds from Mam's emergency card. I figured Tad could help me pay it all back, so it wouldn't matter. And just before I ran upstairs, I added, "Remember, walk as fast as you can to the shop so no one sees you – especially Mo, and *don't* take Kat and Peck inside the shop! Or Mrs Davies will get suspicious."

'Now that it was all happening for real and wasn't just a plan in our heads, Kavi began chewing extra loudly, like a cow in a chewing competition, and Inara started nodding extra fast like a robot that was malfunctioning. I tried not to think about everything that could go wrong, and ran upstairs.

'I don't know how I stopped myself from giving Mam the longest cwtch ever, but I did. Instead I told her I'd see her later, just like normal, and she told me to ask one of the neighbours for help if the box got too heavy to drag to school. I said Inara and Kavi were going to meet me to help and she wasn't to worry – which wasn't really a lie at all. Then I made sure she was super comfortable and had all her favourite chair cushions just how she liked them, and all her medicines too. And taking one long look at her and telling myself everything was going to be OK, I took Kat and Peck and their bags downstairs.

'The second they saw Inara and Kavi in the kitchen, Kat and Peck started squealing, so I rushed them out into the front garden instead of Kavi doing it like we'd planned. Kneeling down, I helped them zip up their coats.

'"Kat . . . Peck . . . I've got to play a game of hide and seek today," I told them, while Kavi nodded at them. "It's a super-important game – for a competition – and if I win, I can help Mam lots and lots and lots. While I'm hiding, you have to listen to Inara and Kavi and do everything they say. And you can't tell anyone that I'm playing either, OK?"

'Kat asked, "Is it a secret like all our top-secret important secrets?"

'I said, "Yup. Just like that."

'"A secret-secret," whispered Peck, as he and Kat looked at each other and made the shushing sign with their little fingers. I tried to say something else but my voice began to wobble like a big blob of jelly – so I reached out and pulled them into a hug instead.

'"I love you both more than anything on the planet," I whispered. Then, pushing them away from me, I told them to stay with Kavi and play the silence game for as long as they could. They always got bored playing that game pretty quickly, but I knew it'd buy me a few minutes.

'In the kitchen, Inara was holding up the tape and scissors and looking green.

'"Ready?" she asked.

'I nodded and, putting on Kavi's cap, climbed into the box. "Close it real tight and proper," I ordered her. "And quickly too. We're running out of time."

'I lowered myself down, feeling like an astronaut who was about to be catapulted into space. Curling myself up into a ball, I looked up at Inara. All the cushions and blankets made it super squashy, so I couldn't really move.

'Inara handed me her lunch box and drink and my inquisitions book. "Come back quick, OK?" she whispered. "And don't get hurt!"

'I looked up one last time and nodded, as the cardboard doors above my head closed shut and everything went dark.

'A few seconds later I heard the sound of tape being stuck across the top and then lots of grunts and groans as the box began to move slowly across the floor. I heard Kavi joining in and pushing me out into the hall, and then a bump as we all made it out through the front door and out on to the street. Then I heard the front door being shut and more grunts and groans and giggles from Kat and Peck as the box was jolted this way and that way. But then after a while everything went still, and I stopped moving. I heard Kavi whispering, "We can't lift it on to the scooters! It's too heavy! What are we going to do?"

'And then, from further away, I heard a van door sliding shut and someone shouting, "What's this then, kids? Need some help?" I thought it was Mr Llewelyn but couldn't be sure.

'Inara's voice spoke. "Yes, please. It's a school project."

'Whoever it was must have lifted me on to the scooters, because I felt a tilt and a shove and then a bump as I landed back down. Kavi said, "Thanks!", and then I was gliding and rattling and bumping over pavements. It's true what they say, you know – when you can't see things, your other senses turn into Spider-Man senses. I could hear Kat and Peck skipping alongside the box, and footsteps and wheels and the engines of cars and trucks and bikes whizzing past and . . . then we stopped moving. I heard Kavi tell Kat and Peck to stay where they were and that if they didn't move he would give them some fruit pastilles. And then there was lots of grunting and bumps again and finally a . . . *beep-boop*! We had made it to Mrs Davies' shop.

'I stayed extra still then, to try and hear as much as I could, but Mrs Davies had the radio on, so it was harder to hear what everyone was saying. I could hear Inara saying ". . . for special . . . day delivery . . ."

'And the sound of Mrs Davies' slippers . . . and a "No . . . we don't . . . iver . . . too big . . . no . . . sheens," and Inara crying out, "It's not . . . oshing machine . . . it's wedding . . . urniture . . . ade by . . . andfather . . . has to . . . today! My mam . . . go today! Pleeeeeease!"

'For a few minutes, all I could hear was the radio and the sound of a million thoughts gushing into my head. Like, what if the box really *was* too big to post? What if Mrs Davies wanted to open it to see what was inside? What if we didn't have enough money? But then suddenly, I heard a "All righ! . . . et me fill in . . . at form," and a *beep-boop!* And then *thud! Thud! THUD!*

'A moment later I heard Mrs Davies' voice again, so close it was like she was trying to get into the box with me. "Frank, take this one, would you?" Through the mini holes I'd made so I could breathe, I saw she was right above me.

'"What is it?" asked a new voice from slightly further away.

'"Wedding gift – made by the bride's grandfather – needs to get there today for a part of the ceremony apparently. It'll have to go express. Chances are low, but can't do more than that."

'"What's with all these other stamps?" The voice had got closer. "They're quite tidy. I might take a picture for—"

'But I never heard the end of Frank's sentence, because the box suddenly shot upwards like a swerving lift. I squeezed myself back into the cushions and held on tight to Inara's lunch box to stop it from rattling.

'Then there were footsteps . . . and a *BANG-BANG!*

The sound of metal doors being slammed shut . . .
and the sound of an engine growling to life as the
ground beneath me began to tremble and shake.

# 17

## Crash Landing

'Have you been on a plane before – like a real one?' I ask.

Sergeant Anita and Georgie both nod.

'I haven't. Not ever. It's always been my dream to go on one flown by a real-life pilot, and to have a real holiday too – just like the real Audrey does in some of her films. Mam used to have lots, she said, before we were born. Her and Tad loved travelling. They went to really far-away countries like Brazil and Norway and East Anglia. But I wouldn't even mind if I didn't go anywhere – just being on the plane would be enough. I've always wanted to try the food. Kavi says plane food is the best food on the planet because the cheese and crackers and food packets and fizzy drinks are all mini, and it's fun to eat mini things when everything around you is rattling and shaking.

'Trying to eat Inara's packed lunch while I was squashed up inside the box is probably the closest I'll ever come to eating anything on a plane. And it wasn't even a bit fun! The straw of the drink kept going up my nose or poking me in the eye because it was too dark to see. And eating a cheese and tomato sandwich in the dark wasn't fun either – all the filling kept shaking and falling out everywhere. It was almost like I was in a washing machine for real – except one that was making me get dirtier instead of cleaner.

'I gave up trying to eat the sandwich after a while – most of it had fallen out anyway and I could feel bits of tomato getting squished on to Mam's cushions. Mo had said Swansea was about three hours away from London, so I knew there was a long time to go before I got to Tad. And since I didn't have a mobile phone or a glow-in-the-dark anything to play with, I closed my eyes and told myself to fall asleep.

'But I didn't know that post never goes straight to the place they're meant to go to. Mrs Davies and Mo didn't tell me that there's lots of places letters and parcels stop at *before* their final destination. So just as I was starting to fall asleep, the shivering and shaking stopped, and everything went super quiet, and then there was a loud clicking sound – like a door was being unlocked, and a voice shouted, "OH! OWAIN! I GOT A FEW PRIORITIES HERE FOR YOU!"

'Then there were lots of noises like *thud*, and *thump*, and *CA-RASH*. And then suddenly I was being pulled out and up and placed on something and moved to somewhere where there was lots of light and the sounds of whirring machines everywhere – like a dozen food processors all going at once. It was so loud I wished I'd brought some ear muffs to put on top of Kavi's scrum cap. Then another voice shouted right above me, "Who's wanting to get a washing machine to London by one o'clock?"

'I looked up through the breathe holes to try and see who the new voice belonged to, but all I could make out was a glimpse of bright-yellow luminous vest.

'"Lucky for our backs it's not a machine,' shouted the first voice again. "Some kind of wedding gift a kid's mam needs sending. Wedding today, or no way Susannah would have allowed it. Saw them – right dwt kids –

down at her shop, begging her. She even knocked a few pounds off so they could afford the postage."

'Both the voices went quiet for a moment and all I could hear was beeping and more loud whirring. And then the new voice said, "Hey, Frank – look at all these stamps. You know who's going to love seeing these, don't you?"

'The Frank voice said, "I'm way ahead of you. Sent him some pictures already, I have. You know he'll be talking about it all day come tomorrow."

'Then they both laughed and there was another beeping sound to the side of me, and the Owain voice said, "Let me know what he says. Anyway, I'll get this lot down to Cardiff on the next one out. Then it'll be in their hands."

'The voices and the high-vis jacket disappeared, and I could feel myself and the box getting lifted and landing on to something hard. I cuddled right up into a ball so that I could be as light as possible, and heard a woman shout, "SAME DAYERS!" as I was plonked down on to something.

'I leaned forward just then to have a look, and saw a metal cage door in front of me. I was in some sort of trolley. And on either side of me were lots of other trolleys filled with hundreds of boxes, all standing in lines that seemed to go on forever and ever.

'I don't know how long I waited, but then suddenly my cage started moving. Someone was pushing me backwards, and there were some loud beeping noises and I was going up, and up, and up and then down. I landed in a lorry whose inside was as long as the longest corridor at school. It was filled with lots of cages that had packages of every shape and size locked behind their prison doors.

'A few seconds after that, the doors of the lorry came rolling down with a long clanging sound and every bit of daylight disappeared.

'I sat and waited again for something else to happen, but for the longest time nothing did. I'm not afraid of the dark usually, but this dark was so pitch black it was different. It was silent and heavy, and made me start to feel as if I didn't exist any more. I had to try really hard not to think about how easy it would be for me to get forgotten about and end up stuck inside the box and on the back of a lorry forever and ever and ever.

'Dr Adeola always tells Mam to breathe in and out slowly when she's in pain or panicking, so I did that. The air holes in my box were too small to let all the heat out, so I was starting to get sweaty and sticky. I wanted to move and stretch my arms and legs but I couldn't. Thinking about it, I should have taken a torch. I never want to be in a place that dark ever again, or that small. I had just started whispering out loud to myself that this was for Mam and that soon I'd be with Tad, when suddenly there were more beeping noises and two loud thumps. That must have been a special "Go!" sign, because the lorry started shaking and moving.

'I was so happy that we were finally on our way, I gave myself a hug. But then a few minutes later I started to get cold – really cold. As if something had come and wrapped a cloak of ice around me. I rubbed my arms and hands and legs and hugged the cushions – but they had turned cold too. My teeth started chattering really bad, so I curled up tight like an armadillo and hugged myself tighter.

'I guess I must have fallen asleep straight after, because the next thing I remember is a really loud beeping noise. I could hear lots of shouting outside, and then the door of the lorry opening. Two hands wearing large grey gloves came towards me and rolled my cage on to a lift. I went down, down, down, to someone wearing a bright-yellow jacket like the ones we have to wear for school trips and was rolled over to another truck – except this one was smaller.

'"These are London bound then, are they?" a voice asked.

'Someone behind me said, "You can bet your sheep they are!" before more beeping noises started and my cage was lifted up on to the truck.

'I couldn't believe it! We were still in Wales – I could tell from the accents. Mam says you can always tell when you're in London because the people are too busy to put any music in their words like we do. That's not – like a bad thing,' I added, looking up to see if Georgie and Sergeant Anita were angry at me for saying that. But they didn't seem to be. 'Anyway, I had already been in the box forever and I wished I was in London already. I couldn't bear the idea of sitting in a ball for who knew how much longer, and feeling that cold again. But I had to – for Mam. I couldn't give up. Not yet.

'The doors to the new truck shut with a noise that went like *KA-KA-KA-KA-KA-KA-KA-KA-KAAAAAAAA-BANG*, and everything became dark again. And this time the engine hummed to life almost straight away. Hoping this journey wouldn't be so long, I squeezed my eyes tight and fell back into a strange kind of sleep where I kept waking up every few minutes to see if I was anywhere yet.

'After what felt like years and years had passed by, I woke up again to the sound of beeps and shouts and trolley wheels, and the sight of red vests and more hands. Feeling my trolley bumping down on to a real floor that wasn't shivering and shaking, I peered through the holes and saw a large red sign with the words: "ROYAL MAIL MOUNT PLEASANT HQ".

'Seeing those words made me scared. I began to worry that maybe I'd been taken to some mountain instead of London.

'But those thoughts left my head the very next second, because my box suddenly got lifted up and pushed on to something that was moving really fast. I tried to see where I was – but things were whizzing past me in a blur. It took my brain a few seconds to catch up with my eyes and tell me that I was on a giant conveyor belt.

'I wanted to see where it was going. So I leaned to the side of my box and pushed my eyes as close to the holes as possible. I could hear beeps and bumps and could see a large machine ahead of me, with lots of lights on it . . . and boxes were going into it like they were heading into a square-shaped tunnel . . .

'And that was when it happened! I must have leaned too much, or maybe the belt was moving too quickly, but suddenly my box began to tip. And before I could stop it, it lunged and flew right off the belt, landing with a crash on to the floor.

'I was upside down on my head when the sound of sirens began to scream and the whirring buzz of the belt stopped. Some of my things – like my inquisitions book and one of Mam's doctor letters so that Tad could see how serious it all was – had fallen out of my pockets and landed near my head. But worse – *much* worse – my legs had gone straight and smashed right through the bottom of the box; I could feel them kicking in the air. I knew that meant *everyone* could see me and that I had to run. So I rolled around until I was on my side, and punched and ripped and pushed my way out of the box.

'When I stood up, people in blue uniforms and yellow jackets were rushing towards me from every direction. I didn't know what else to do, so I began to run, just as fast I could, leaving everything I had behind me.'

# 18

## The Ghost Train Rider

'You must have been absolutely terrified,' says Georgie, looking worried. Sergeant Anita nods in agreement.

'I was,' I say, sitting up straighter in my chair. 'I'd never been chased by that many grown-ups before – and all of them were shouting things like, "HEY!" and "OI!" and "STOP HER!" It was well scary, but I knew I couldn't get caught before I made it to Tad's! So I made myself run faster and zigged and zagged and pushed and dived and skidded my way past all the giant letter machines and the postwomen and postmen reaching out to grab me. I didn't know where I was running to – I was just heading to whatever door I could see. But every time I got close to one, someone would suddenly appear right in front of it like a bright human traffic cone, trying to catch me.

'I think I shouted "LEAVE ME ALONE!" lots of times, but nobody would. I kept moving faster and faster – so fast that everyone became all blurry and my eyes couldn't see anything any more. I nearly got grabbed so many times, but I just kept ducking and pushing everyone away, and there were at least two postmen who fell down trying to catch me and squeaked right across the floor instead!

'Then I saw it – this huge gap in the wall and some stairs leading straight down. No one seemed to be near it, so I ran towards it so hard that I couldn't even feel my legs.

'I was nearly there when a man wearing a shiny suit with even shinier buttons jumped out in front of me with his arms and legs stretched out like a net. "YOUNG LADY! STOP RIGHT THERE!" he shouted. His belly was huge and bouncy, and it gave me an idea. I ran straight towards him like a dart speeding towards a bullseye, but right at the last second I dived through his legs and out the other side behind him.

'My plan worked – because two seconds later I heard a huge crash! Everyone who had been chasing me had run straight into him.

'I carried on running right towards the doorway, thinking I had made it, when a hand came out of nowhere, grabbed my arm and swung me into a stop.

'For a second, when I looked up at his face, I thought it was Mo – he had nearly the exact same moustache. But it wasn't. So I kicked him in the leg and the second he let go of me I ran through the doorway and down the stairs . . . and another flight of stairs . . . and another and another. But the more I ran down, the more there seemed to be, and they got narrower and narrower too, until finally they ended in what looked like the entrance to an underground cave. In front of it was a tall metal fence, with a sign on it that said "AUTHORISED PERSONNEL ONLY".

'I tried to look for somewhere else to go, but there was no other way out – really there wasn't. The only way was back up the stairs, and I could already hear the echoes of footsteps running down the stairs behind me, getting louder and closer. I had to keep going – I just had to! So I went up to the fence and tried to push myself through its gaps. There were five whole seconds when my head got stuck and I thought I wouldn't make it, but then I pushed and pulled so hard that I fell out on to the other side. That's when I scraped my knees and ripped everything, see.'

Standing up, I show Sergeant Anita and Georgie the plasters and the holes in the knees of my dungarees. Just in case they hadn't seen them properly before.

'Ouch,' says Sergeant Anita. 'That must have hurt quite a bit.'

'And my hands too,' I say, showing her the scrapes and grazes on my palms. 'But it wasn't so bad. I could still run. And the ambulance doctors that saw me after you caught me said my new skin would be back in no time. It still stings though.'

'Did you cry when you fell down, Audrey?' asks Georgie. 'I think I would have done.'

I shake my head. 'I wanted to, I think, but I didn't have time. The pain screamed really loudly, but the screams inside my head were louder. They told me I had to get up and run, or I'd never be able to get to Tad! So I kept going as fast as I could down the tunnel. After a few seconds, I could see bright-yellow glowing lights getting bigger and bigger in front of me and I thought I could hear the wheels of a train. You can always tell the sound of a train – they go *CLACKETY-CLACK,*

*CLACKETY-CLACK*. But I wasn't sure if it was coming from in front of me or from behind me. Either way, I just kept running.

'But when I got to the end of the tunnel, there *wasn't* a train at all – there were just two postmen standing next to each other on a very short platform. One had a tall pile of grey sacks next to him, and the other was standing next to an empty cage trolley – just like the one I had been put in on the Royal Mail lorry. In front of them was a rail track – but no train. A few steps away from them, right at the end of the tiny platform, was a large metal control pad with lots of orange, green and red lights flashing on and off.

'That was when I *really* wanted to cry, because I had reached the end of the tunnel, and instead of finding a way out I was even more trapped. I hid in the shadows for a few seconds, trying to be silent so that the postmen wouldn't hear me. In a minute or two, everyone who was chasing me would find me – and I'd be stopped from reaching Tad once and for all. Or the two men in front would turn around and see me and press a siren button.

'I was trying to think about what to do when a voice

blasted out across the air. It said, "*Tchk!* Red to Whitechapel . . . incoming. Over. *Tchk!*"

'The short postman in front of me grabbed the walkie-talkie on his belt and replied, "*Tchk!* Ready for incoming and deposit to Whitechapel. Over. *Tchk!*"

'Then something really tidy happened. The moment the last "*tchk!*" had finished, the *clackety-clack* noise I'd heard started to get louder and louder and suddenly a train appeared – a real one! But it was nothing like any train I've ever seen before! It was so small that it looked like a ghost-train ride at the fairground – except it was bright red and had a shiny glass roof and "Royal Mail" in large yellow letters on the side. I watched it pulling in and realised that, just like a ghost train, it didn't have a driver.

'The tall postman grabbed his trolley cage and said something like, "Here we go – let's see who wins this time."

'And the shorter postman said, "No way you're beating me, Joe," and grabbed as many grey bags as he could. I knew right away they were going to have a race of some kind.

'When the ghost train came to a stop, the glass roofs

to all the carriages flew open. It was magic – like seeing a row of super-shiny see-through boxes suddenly being unlocked by an invisible magician. I couldn't see what was inside the carriages, but there definitely weren't any people. There didn't even seem to be any seats!

'Shouting "GO!", the shorter postman started throwing all the grey sacks he had, two by two, into one of the empty carriages.

'And the other postman – the tall one with the cage – began leaning over and unloading bright-blue sacks from the other carriage, and throwing them into his cage trolley.

'The voice from the walkie-talkie boomed out again and said, "*Tchk!* Thirty seconds to departure for Whitechapel. All loading and unloading to be complete in thirty. Over. *Tchk!*"

'The tall postman shouted, "Be over long before then, mate!", and the shorter one made a grunting noise and started grabbing four sacks at a time.

'Suddenly I knew what I had to do – there was no other way out. I didn't know where "White Chapel" was, but it didn't sound like anywhere in Wales – so I figured it was in England – maybe even in London.

And anyway, any place that was a chapel would be sure to help me. It was better than getting caught at Mount Not-So-Pleasant.

'I couldn't do anything right away, because the postmen in front of me were still unloading and loading the sacks. But then the *Tchk*-voice came out of the walkie-talkie again. "Ten seconds to departure. Over. *Tchk!*" At the same time, from behind me, a loud, scary voice shouted out, "THERE SHE IS!"

'Knowing I couldn't wait any longer, I pushed myself out of the shadows, and ran and ran and ran as fast as I could towards the train. Before I could reach it, the glass roofs started to close shut, and both the postmen had turned towards me and were stretching out their hands . . .

'I lunged right past the short postman and, jumping up with every muscle I had, dived straight through the tiny gap between the roof and the carriage – and landed right on top of the sharp pile of grey sacks it had been filled with.

'A second later the glass roof clicked shut, and the train began to move. I sat up just in time to see the faces of the two postmen staring back at me with their mouths wide open, and all the people who had been chasing me flooding the platform. For a single moment I could see every single one of their faces clearly, before they all disappeared into a tube of darkness, like a painting being sucked up by a hoover. In their place, lots of lights whizzed above my head, faster and faster and faster.

'I knew I was safe as long as I was on the train, so I lay down and quickly tried to make a new plan for what to do when the train stopped. It was only then that I realised I was lying on a big pile of pointy envelopes and that I was on a real-life, extra-special Royal Mail underground train! One that carried letters instead of people – real, actual letters with lots of stamps from everywhere! Mo and Mrs Davies had never mentioned anything like it, so I thought maybe they didn't know it existed. I couldn't wait to tell them about it then . . . although they'll probably never talk to me again after today.

'While I was lying on them, the sacks gave me an idea. I knew I had to stay hidden at the next station, so I dug myself down as much as I could, and even found an empty sack near me – this one,' I say, holding up the grey sack in my hand to show Sergeant Anita and Georgie. 'I covered myself with it and waited for all the flashing lights to slow down.

'My plan was to wait until the mail people at the next station started to unload the sacks on top of me. Then, when they weren't looking, I would sneak out and make a run for the chapel. We have loads of chapels in Wales, see, and everyone in them is always super nice, so I hoped it'd be the same in a London one. And once I got there, I'd ask someone to help me find Tad's address.

'And then . . . and then, well, you know what happened next,' I say, reaching the end of my story and looking up at Sergeant Anita.

Leaning forward, she gives me a smile. 'I do,' she says. 'But for the record, Audrey, why don't you end it for us? I'd like to hear it from your perspective.'

'OK,' I say. 'Erm . . . I was lying down and hiding under this sack. Let me show you.'

Getting off my chair, I lay down on the floor, making my body extra straight, and pull the grey sack over me. Speaking through the sack, I say, 'I lay down like this – but imagine lots of sacks on top of me. I couldn't see the lights or anything any more, but I could feel the train starting to slow down.

'That was when I started getting real scared again, but I got ready anyway. And then I heard the doors hissing open – like *HA-AH-Sssssssssssssssssssssssssssss*. I made my body go even *more* still and waited for a postman to shout, "Here we go" and for the sacks on top of me to start to get taken. But instead, it was all silent.

'Right up until someone shouted: "WE KNOW YOU'RE IN THERE! COME OUT WITH YOUR HANDS UP!"'

# 19

## Return to Sender

'You can get up off the floor now, Audrey,' says Sergeant Anita, her voice sounding wobbly.

Pushing the sack from my face, I get up and go back to my chair. Sergeant Anita's lips are twitching again, and Georgie has a hand over her mouth and her shoulders are shaking. Wondering what's so funny, I finish my story.

'And then at least a hundred police officers came to catch me, and the ambulance doctors put that stinging liquid on my knees, and then they brought me here. Where I met you and you . . . and, well, that's it.'

Sergeant Anita looks at me for a few moments, and then slowly closes her evidence book. 'Audrey, I think that may be the most thorough confession this constabulary has ever heard. Thank you for sharing your side of the story with us.'

'Yes,' says Georgie, giving my hand a squeeze. 'You did a deeply fantastic job in recounting everything that led you here.'

'Thanks,' I say, feeling proud that I had remembered so much. 'So . . . what will happen now?' I ask, trying to sound brave as I pull the grey sack close to my chest.

'Well . . .' Sergeant Anita looks at her watch. 'Hopefully you'll be heading home soon. And tomorrow I'll relay our report to the chief officers at the Royal Mail, so they can decide what they want to do with the information, and whether the damages they have incurred can be retrieved, despite the unusualness of the situation.'

'Damages?' I look down at my knees, wondering what else I've damaged besides them.

'Yes, damages,' says Sergeant Anita. 'You see, Audrey, when you fell from the conveyer belt you triggered alarms, which shut that whole facility down. And then there were also injuries to personnel, and the underground rail you were on stopped for over an hour – which will have set postal works across the country back by quite a bit. Important letters and packages that were meant to get to places by certain times will have been delayed, which may frustrate the people who sent them. They'll ask for answers and maybe even financial compensation. The Royal Mail has to try and find ways to rectify quite a few situations, and perhaps speak to Mo, and Mrs Davies and Frank and the other postal workers you mentioned too – just to see if they were aware of anything suspicious about your box or if they had any hint as to your intentions. You see, you should have been stopped long before you actually posted yourself. Your box would have felt unusual and heavy, and the fact that children were trying to post it should have raised alarms – especially with Mrs Davies. It's every postmaster's and postmistress's job to ensure nothing dangerous or – *alive* – is ever mailed.'

'Oh no,' I whisper, looking down at the grey sack. I hadn't realised I had made so many things go wrong – it was the dominoes all over again, like in Mrs Davies' shop the day I had got caught.

'It wasn't their fault,' I say, louder. 'Definitely not Mrs Davies'! Inara and Kavi are really good at acting! Even I didn't know they could act that good.'

Leaning towards the black box so that it, and whoever was going to listen to it, could hear me properly, I state clearly, 'Mrs Davies and all those Royal Mail people are innocent. And just to say, I didn't mean to kick that postman in the leg. Or jump on that train. And if it's top secret, I promise I won't tell anyone I was on it – or that I even saw it! I just wanted to get to Tad so he could help my mam, and keep *Them* away from us forever, that's all. You understand, don't you?'

Worried, I look up at Sergeant Anita. 'Will you give *Them* your report too – so they know I didn't mean it? And can you put in it that Mam is the best mam on the planet, even though she can't do everything and needs my help sometimes and to please, please not to take me and Kat and Peck away from her? Maybe *They* could even find Tad for me and ask him to help us, or help Mam get everything she needs instead? That would be better, wouldn't it – wouldn't it?'

'Calm down, Audrey,' says Georgie, reaching out and putting her hands around my shoulders. It feels nice and warm, like a shawl. 'Nobody is trying to take you away from your mum.'

'You don't know that,' I say. 'What about the spies

across the road? How come they were spying on us if they weren't *Them*?'

Sergeant Anita has been nodding slowly while I talk, and when I finish she says, 'Audrey, I have made a very special note to inform the Welsh constabulary of the situation with the house across the street, and I will personally be asking them to check it out as soon as they can. Just to make sure everything is OK there. All right? It's highly unlikely a local authority team would set up a sting operation like that – and for this length of time. Not without notifying a range of authorities. So if – IF – we find anything suspect, or indeed confirm your fears, I will let you know.'

'Really? Promise?'

'Really,' promises Sergeant Anita. 'Any allegations of spying or – as your friends Kavi and Inara suspect – erm, planned robberies are things we take rather seriously. We'll ask for all the records to be checked out thoroughly. If you don't hear back from us, it's because we haven't found anything to be worried about. OK?' She opens her mouth to say something else, but before she can, three knocks bang on the door. It opens to reveal another police officer, who's so short and

243

round he looks like a smartly dressed penguin. I recognise him as one of the policemen from the platform at Whitechapel who was waiting to arrest me there.

'Ma'am, the pick-up is here,' he says, looking over at me and giving me a friendly smile.

'Good. Please let them know we're on our way.'

'Is it my tad?' I ask, feeling excited. I haven't seen him in over two years, and I bet he looks the same, even though I don't – I must have grown at least four inches. I wonder if he'll recognise me right away. 'Did you go to his address? Was he there? That's who's come, isn't it?' I ask the officer.

But he only looks at the floor and leaves the room with a quick shuffle.

Sergeant Anita leans into the black machine. 'Interview terminated at . . . seven forty-nine p.m., Thursday thirty-first March.' Clicking a button on the black box so that the red lights switch off, she smiles and says, 'Let's go and see, shall we? Follow me, please, Audrey.'

I jump down off my chair, leaving the grey postman's sack on it. I don't need it any more. Georgie takes one of my hands and we both follow Sergeant Anita back out through all the offices and rooms. I'm starting to feel all jumpy and excited, so I skip beside her, my skips getting higher and bouncier the closer we get to the place Sergeant Anita had met me before. Tad is going to be there – and he'll think how tall I've become, and I'll tell him all about everything I'd done to reach him, and why he needs to stop being so lost and come and help Mam out. My plan had still worked, even with all the things that had gone wrong with it.

As the huge glass elevators and sparkling lights and bobbing police hats come into view again, I hear a cry.

'AUDREY!'

I stop. It can't be – it just can't! I search the direction it's come from, my eyes hungry to look everywhere at once. And then I see her.

'MAM!' I cry back. Ripping my hand out of Georgie's, I run into her arms. Mam is here! In London! I can feel her and her hair and her coat and her skin so I'm not imagining it!

'Oh, Audrey . . . Audrey . . .' she whispers. 'What did you do, my darling girl?'

Stepping back from her, I look up for a second and, wiping my tears away, rub my eyes extra hard and then open them again. She's still here. It's real.

'Mam – how did you get here? Is it Tad? Did he bring you?'

I look around to find him, but instead another face I never expected to see pops out from behind her.

'Good evening, little madam! What's all this about then, eh?' it says.

'MO!' I cry out, as he steps forward and gives me a cwtch too.

'Well, you do know how to keep us on our toes, that's a fact,' says Mo, smiling his huge smile. 'Mailing yourself to London. You sure do beat all the kids in Wales, Audrey!'

'*You* brought Mam?' I ask. 'Did . . . did anyone else come too?' I look behind him to make sure I haven't missed someone else, but all I can see are lots of police officers looking our way, watching us like we're one of Mam's TV dramas.

Mo looks confused and shakes his head. 'No – it's just the two of us. Kat and Peck are with Mrs Lumley. Don't worry, little madam – they're being well looked after.'

'You're a good friend, Mo. I don't know what we'd do without you,' says Mam, leaning heavily on her canes.

'But – but where's Tad?' I ask, still looking around.

Mam goes quiet for a second. 'He's not here, darling,' she says quietly. Her face looks like it's in pain. Except this isn't a pain caused by her bones, I can tell. It's something else – something new.

Mam leans down to me, placing her face closer to mine. From behind her I can see Mo looking down at me sadly.

'Audrey, tell me, darling, why did you try and *mail* yourself to him? Why?'

'Because – he – he needs to help us!' I say quietly, feeling my whole face start to catch on fire. 'He needs to help us get all the things the doctor ordered – like the wheelchair and the lift and the bathroom sweet . . .' I explain, my voice getting louder as I go. 'I thought I'd ask him – just like we ask him for all the things we want at Christmas. He always gets us everything, doesn't he? I thought he could help us get everything we need for you too, and that way we'll be safe.'

I don't know what I'm expecting, but Mam looking as if I've hurt her heart isn't one of them.

Wiping away the tears that have made her whole cheek wet, she reaches out and touches my face. I haven't felt her fingers on my cheeks in a long time, and now my cheeks start getting wet too, and my heartbeat thumps and kicks louder and louder. I know it's because it doesn't want my ears to hear what she's going to say. But it doesn't work. I can still hear everything.

'Oh, Audrey . . . it's not your tad who gets those presents,' she whispers. 'It's . . . it's Mo. He – he gets everyone on our street to do that for us. Your tad . . . he has a new family now. He – he doesn't want anything to do with us. Not because he doesn't love you and Peck and Kat, but because it's all too painful for him. He just – he just couldn't cope with seeing me like this. That's all. Some people aren't as strong as they want to be . . .'

Mam says more words after that, but I don't hear them. My fingers and toes have gone ice cold, and a loud ringing sounds in my ears. Of *course* he hadn't bought us presents at Christmas! Of *course* none of those things were from him. All the neighbours knowing who I was when I'd done the Welsh Inquisition makes sense now. Of *course* they knew – they all knew, except *me*. And of *course* Tad has a new family. And of *course* they're better than we are . . .

I don't know what happens next. All I know is my insides feel like a sheet of glass someone has smashed into a million pieces that no one will ever be able to put back together again.

But then someone pulls me into their arms and stops me from breaking.

I don't know how long I stand with my face buried in Mam's chest. All I know is that for the first time ever I let myself cry as much as I want to. Even though I'm scared of everything that might happen now because of all the things I got wrong, I don't want to be in any other place except right here, with my mam's heartbeat wrapped around me like an envelope that has been sealed, holding me and her inside it.

# 20

## The Letter with the Golden Stamp

Sometimes, when a big adventure goes wrong in ways even your imagination couldn't have imagined, trying to get back to normal life and pretending that you're OK when you're not can feel like the hardest thing in the world. I know, because in the days after my journey to London nothing was quite the same as it was before.

On the drive home from the not-really-in-Scotland-or-in-a-yard Scotland Yard office, I didn't want to talk. Not even to Mam or Mo, even though they were the two people in the whole of the Milky Way who knew the most about me – besides Inara and Kavi and Kat and Peck, of course. And now maybe Mrs Davies too. I couldn't have talked even if I had wanted to, because the egg that usually got stuck in my throat felt like it had been replaced by a full-sized chicken whose feathers were tickling my insides so much they made my eyes water.

Mam was silent as well – I could tell she was trying to pretend she wasn't in pain from having to sit in the car for such a long time. Mo must have guessed we both wanted to be quiet, because instead of asking me a million questions, he told us stories about all the trouble he had got into as a young boy in the place where he lived when he was little – the one on the special Dominican Republic stamp with all the palm trees on it. I listened at first, but then the thoughts in my head got so loud they filled my ears like big blobs of earwax, and I couldn't hear anything except them after a while. Every single one of them was telling me how much I had failed everyone. How I had failed Kat and Peck by thinking Tad was the one who had sent us all those presents, and that he was the someone we needed to save us. And how I had failed Inara and Kavi by falling out of the box. And how I had failed Mrs Davies by telling Sergeant Anita and Georgie her name. And how I had failed Mo by losing all the precious stamps he had got me . . . and how I'd even failed people I had never met, who had needed their post by the next day.

But worst of all, I had failed Mam. In every single way. I had to face it now: I couldn't save her or any of us from *Them*. Not any more. Not when there was absolutely no one else who could help us in the way I thought Tad could have. And not when, on top of all my lifting shops and my little black book too, I had told the police everything. It was my turn to feel lost now. I felt more lost than I bet even Tad ever did.

After what felt like a long, long time in the car, Mo came to a stop. The rain was so heavy the wipers on his car were going extra fast. They looked like two stick people dancing to a super-fast beat. I looked up at the foggy window next to me, splattered with drops of rain and spots of light, and saw the hazy shadow of the house opposite ours. The one that would be happy I had failed so badly.

'Audrey, wait here a minute while I get your mam to the door,' said Mo, so gently I could barely hear him. He jumped out of the car, popped open a giant red umbrella and helped Mam on to her feet on the pavement. I watched them slowly walk to the door and heard Mo knocking his usual three knocks on it before they disappeared inside.

'Ready?'

I looked up at the suddenly opened door, and Mo's smile and the big red umbrella, but I didn't move. I didn't want everything to end like this . . . I didn't want to go home – not yet. And even if I had wanted to move, I just couldn't. My legs had turned to tree trunks that wanted to stay rooted to the car.

Mo leaned down. 'What's happening here then, little madam?' he asked.

I shrugged and carried on looking down at my knees.

'You know, it's all going to be OK, Audrey. I know it doesn't feel like it, but it will, I promise. These things always have a way of working themselves out. Believe you me.'

I didn't believe him. Not even a little bit. But still, his words made my legs feel like legs again, so I moved them and me out of the car and into the house.

That night, after Kat and Peck had been ordered to let go of Mrs Lumley's dog and been put to bed, and everyone left, Mam told me we both had to go to bed too. I wanted to sleep in her room – just to make sure she was OK, but she shook her head at me and said, 'Not tonight, Audrey. I need some time to think.'

The way she said it scared me, even though she gave me a kiss on top of my head as she said it. But this wasn't a happy kiss. It was a sad one, and it felt like a weight I would have to carry forever. I carried it to bed and, curling myself up into a ball like I had done inside the box, I cried myself to sleep.

\* \* \*

The next day, lots of strange things began to happen.

First, Mam told me that Dr Adeola was coming. I told her I wanted to stay so I could help and tidy the house, but Mam was stricter than she'd ever been before and told me I had to go to school, even though I was so sleepy. She gave me the scariest of all her looks and said it in a voice that made me know there was no point arguing.

Then Mo didn't knock on our door at the usual time. In fact, when the post did eventually come, there was no knock at all. Just a letter pushed through the letterbox. I ran to the door and threw it open as soon as the letter came through, but instead of Mo standing on the other side, there was a postwoman with bright-red hair curled into a bun and freckles all across her face. I asked her where Mo was, and she said she didn't know who that was, but that maybe he had been stationed in another area.

That made me think that the police in London had taken him to be interviewed or maybe the Royal Mail were taking him away from me forever as a punishment for breaking their machines and riding the secret underground train. So on my way to school I ran with Kat and Peck to Mrs Davies' shop to see if she knew anything. But she wasn't there behind her counter either. In her place was the lady called Nessa who had caught me and made everything crash to the floor. I was so scared at seeing her, I didn't ask her anything at all and ran straight back out on to the street. Mrs Davies had been taken too!

Then at school, Kavi and Inara weren't in the playground before the bell rang. I looked everywhere for them and asked Nutan and Larry and Angie and even Fatima if they'd seen them. But they all shrugged and Larry said, 'Maybe they're running late?' I knew that couldn't be it – Kavi might sometimes be late by a few minutes, but Inara never was. And for them both to be late at the same time had never happened before. There was always one of them in the playground waiting for me. I waited and waited, even after the bell rang, but they still didn't show.

When I finally got to class, Mrs Li wasn't beside the whiteboard either. In her place was a substitute teacher called Mr Monaghan, who kept clapping his hands after every sentence. Mrs Li had never taken a day off before, so the whole class immediately began whispering about what might have happened to her. Fabian said that maybe her car had crashed into a sheep and she was in jail, and Angie said everyone was being too dramatic and she had probably just gone cliff-diving and hit her head on a rock, and Nutan said Mrs Li was just playing an April fool's joke on us. I knew they were all wrong and that the police had taken her too.

Then at lunchtime, like magic, Inara and Kavi appeared in the playground together, dropped off by their parents. Screaming out their names at the top of my lungs, I ran over and we all hugged and jumped up and down together. I could tell the whole playground was looking at us, but I didn't care! I was so happy and relieved they were back and hadn't been taken away forever that I could have hugged and jumped all day.

Hurrying to our favourite corner, we told each other everything that had happened the day before. It turned out that while I was being interviewed by Sergeant Anita and Georgie in London, *they* were being interviewed by the Swansea police! It was Mrs Li who had rung all the alarm bells first.

'Mrs Li rang your mam to ask where you were, see,' explained Inara. 'You know, when you didn't show up for school. And then when she found out you weren't at home and your mam found out you weren't here, Mr Garcia came and got us out of class to see if we knew.'

'We said we didn't know anything for as long as we could,' said Kavi. 'But then our mams and tads got called and we all had to go to the police station. And that's where we heard about you running on to that train and everyone chasing you. That sounded well awesome, that did,' he added, looking impressed.

'So when did you tell them you posted me in the box?' I ask.

'We didn't! It was Mo! He figured out you'd mailed yourself to your tad!' said Kavi. 'He's well clever.'

'Because of all the stamps you stuck on the box, see! Someone had sent him a picture when you were getting mailed, and he instantly knew it was you. So then *he* called your mam and the police and told them he knew where you were heading,' said Inara, grabbing my arm and squeezing it extra hard.

'The stamps,' I whispered to myself, shaking my head. 'They were supposed to be my lucky stamps but instead they helped me get caught. So that's why the post people were taking pictures of the box – to send them to Mo! They know he collects stamps too!'

Inara and Kavi nodded at me.

'But hold on – if you were being interviewed yesterday by the police, then where were you both this morning?' I asked.

Both Kavi and Inara gave each other a funny look, before Kavi said, 'Nowhere,' and Inara added quickly, 'Mr Garcia, er – said we could have the morning off – you know, after being with the police and things so late.'

Kavi nodded vigorously, which convinced me they were both hiding something. Mr Garcia never let anyone take time off from school. Not even Rodriguez, his own son, had been allowed to stay home when he broke his arm. There was no way he'd be happy to let Kavi and Inara sleep in after we'd all done something so illegal the police had to interview us.

But before I could try and find out where Inara and Kavi had really been, Fatima and Fred and Carey popped up behind us and began asking if it was true that we'd all spent the night in jail in Swansea police station because I had tried to travel to London in a box.

'My dad knows everyone important in town,' said Fatima, swinging her plaits around. 'Even the head of the Welsh Post Offices. He had his face on the Welsh Rugby collectors' pack last year, remember? So I know everything, see!'

Inara told her she couldn't know everything because it was top-secret confidential information, but then more and more people began coming up to ask questions, and before I could stop him, Kavi began telling everyone that it was true – we'd all been to the police, and that I really had been in a box. But then Inara said it was for a talent competition so I could win a ten-thousand-pound prize, and that even though

I hadn't won it I had come close. I knew she made it up so that Mam and Tad could stay my secret, and it made me want to hug her forever.

By home-time the whole school had heard that I'd tried to mail myself to London to win a million pounds for a game show, and that Fatima now thought me and Kavi and Inara were cool – which meant we really must be. Inara and Kavi acted out our make-believe story so many times that even I started to believe some of it and feel cooler too.

The next morning Mrs Li and Mrs Davies were back. They didn't say why they'd been away, but I guessed they'd gone to be interviewed by Sergeant Anita too. I said sorry to them for getting them into trouble with the police and the Royal Mail, and they both said it was OK so long as I didn't do anything like it ever again. I promised I wouldn't and they both gave me a cwtch, which made me feel a bit better.

The only person who still wasn't back was Mo. He wasn't at the door on Saturday, or even on the Monday – the lady with the red hair was still delivering our mail. I wished I could ask Mam if she knew where he was, but she was still being quiet. I knew she was in pain after that long journey to come and get me – I could see she was struggling more and more with the stairs, but that she was trying not to show it. So I didn't feel like I could ask her anything.

But then at exactly eight fifteen on Friday morning, seven whole days after we had got back from London, three knocks echoed through the house.

'MAM! IT'S MO! IT'S MO!' I cried. Kat and Peck squealed and ran behind me so quickly that we all nearly crashed into the door before I could open it.

It *was* Mo. Standing where he always stood, and smiling just like he always smiled! Before he could say a word, I jumped over to him and gave him a huge hug, which made him start to laugh and Kat and Peck giggle.

'Hello, little madam! Miss me much?'

I stepped back and nodded, and then noticed he wasn't alone. Mrs Davies was standing behind him – and Dr Adeola too. I gave them both a confused wave.

'Is your mam downstairs, Audrey?' asked Mo.

I shook my head.

'You may want to go and get her, just as quickly as you can. It's rather urgent.'

I nodded and turned to run back upstairs, my heart

giving me warning beats. What was urgent? And why was Dr Adeola here? *And* Mrs Davies? But before I had reached the staircase, Mam appeared. She had been slowly making her way down already.

'All right, Maya?' asked Mo.

Mam nodded, and for the first time since we had arrived back from London, gave me a real smile.

'Are we through?' she asked.

Mo and Mrs Davies and Dr Adeola all smiled and nodded together, before looking over at me.

'Right. Here we go then,' said Mo, taking a deep breath.

'Miss Audrey. It gives me the greatest pleasure to be able to deliver two things to you today. First . . .'

Turning around, he took something from Mrs Davies. It was a box – and on it was my address and a very large red sticker that said 'PRIORITY'.

'Open it,' said Mo, holding it for me.

Grabbing one side of the large blue tape that was running across the top, I ripped it off, making the lid spring open.

'MY STAMPS!' I cried out. 'And – and MAM! Your GLOVES! And Kavi's SCRUM HAT! And – and my inquisition book!' The box had everything I thought I might never see again. And on top of it all, was a single white card with a picture of a police shield and a crown on top of it. I picked it up and read the words:

As promised.
Take care of yourself, Audrey, and say a warm
hello to your mum and Mo for me.
Kindest regards, Anita X


'That's not all,' said Mo, putting the box down on the floor. 'There's something else too.'

And with a tip of his cap, Mo reached into his Royal Mail bag, and took out a long, cream-coloured envelope with a golden stamp shimmering from one of its corners.

I stared at my own name printed out across the front of the envelope. I'd never received a letter to just me before, all typed out in tidy black typewriter letters. Even birthday cards from my grandparents had always had Mam's name on them, never mine.

Trying to stop my hands from shaking, I turned the envelope over and carefully ripped the V-shaped flap wide open.

Miss Audrey Morisot

33 Swan Terrace

Abertawe

SA2 7PZ CYMRU

The Light of Wales Awards
Wales Millennium Centre
Bute Place
Cardiff CF10 5AL

Miss Audrey Morisot
33 Swan Terrace
Abertawe
SA2 7PZ

7th April

Dear Miss Audrey Morisot,

On behalf of The Light of Wales (Goleuni Cymru) Awards, in partnership with the Welsh Government Young People's Awards, I am writing to offer you my heartfelt congratulations on your being voted the winner of BOTH this year's Exceptional Young Carer Award and this year's Bravery Award. Llongyfarchiadau!

Following an initial submission by Mr Mo Hernandez, recent further nominations have been received ahead of the final deadline from the following people: Ms Maya Morisot; Mrs Angelica Davies; Dr Anthony Adeola; Ms Josie Lumley; Mr Craig Llewelyn; Mr Rayyan Ghosh; Mr Jahangir and Mrs Rujina Miah; Ms Felicity Niamh; Mr Fred F. Stone; Miss Sona Thakrar; the Sinha family inclusive of Kavi Sinha; the Begum family, inclusive of Inara Begum; Mrs Hanh Li; Mr Davey Garcia, together with a late submission by Sergeant Anita Anand of the Metropolitan Police. These have been accepted fully by all members of our joint boards, and key persons interviewed.

This year, thanks to our generous sponsors, we invite you to accept the following prizes included as part of your awards package:

- Attendance for you, your family and four selected friends at a star-studded celebration at the Wales Millennium Centre, Cardiff, where you will receive your awards from international Oscar-winning actor and son of Wales Mr Anthony Jones. Transport and overnight accommodation included.
- Automatic acceptance into any drama, dance,

theatre or counselling programme delivered by organisations affiliated with Young Carers of Cymru.

- Invitation to join the Young Carers of Cymru holiday and adventurers' programme for all your family.
- A cash prize of £1,000.

Please complete the forms overleaf with the assistance of an adult, indicating whether you wish to accept these awards and the prizes offered, and return to my teams in the SAE included, no later than 1st June.

I send our heartiest congratulations to you again, Audrey. And I look forward to meeting you in person soon.

Yours,

*Ms J. Amber-Lee*

Ms Jacqueline Amber-Lee
WELSH FIRST MINISTER

# 21

## On the Other Side of the Street

I stared and stared at the letter, trying to stop the page from shaking but I couldn't – my hands wouldn't let me. I could hear Mam reading out loud everyone's names and all the things I had won as she leaned on her canes, and Mo crying out, 'We did it – right in the nick of time too!' and Mrs Lumley's dog barking as it came to join us with her . . . and Mr Ghosh looking over the fence and asking 'Did it happen?' . . . and Kat crying out 'HOLIDAAAAAY!' . . . and Peck hugging my leg . . . but it all seemed to be happening far away, in a place wrapped in invisible cotton wool.

A thousand pounds! One whole thousand pounds! I could buy Mam's wheelchair – the fanciest one I could find! And ask Mr Llewelyn if he could build

Mam's sweet bathroom if we had anything left over! But then . . . then I remembered how much trouble I had got everyone into – and how I wasn't a hero carer at all . . .

'But – but I'm a THIEF,' I said, looking up at Mam and Mo and everyone. 'I – I'm a thief . . . and I don't deserve this,' I repeated, my throat hurting at having to push out the truth in front of so many people.

Mam shook her head. 'My darling, you took food to stop us going hungry,' she said quietly. 'That's not your fault. It's *my* fault for not realising that you thought it was your job to provide for us. And it's the fault of all the people in power who have forgotten there are lots and lots of people like us who aren't quite as lucky or healthy as they are. You are *my* hero, Audrey. And you're a hero to Kat and Peck and everyone else too. And now, thanks to Mo and Mrs Davies and everyone's beautiful efforts, everyone else in Wales will know that now. I promise I'll look into getting the local food bank to help us, so you don't have to worry so much. And you can use your money to pay off everyone in your black book, and make a fresh start with whatever you have left over. How about that?'

My heart stopped beating for three whole beats. 'You – you know about my black book?' I asked quietly.

Mam nodded and rested her head on top of mine. 'I found it on Thursday,' she said quietly. 'After Mrs Li called to tell me you were missing, I rang Mrs Davies and Mrs Lumley here to help me search for any clue you might have left behind as to where you'd gone. And that's when we found it.'

I wiped away the tears that were pouring down my cheeks. Mam being so quiet all this time made sense now. 'I'm sorry,' I whispered to her, and everyone too.

'We know you are,' said Mrs Davies and Mo and Mam together.

'You're ours, Audrey, and we're mighty proud of you,' said Mrs Lumley, ignoring the fact that Kat and Peck were cuddling her dog so hard it was squeaking instead of barking. 'Everyone on this street is. And we'll always be here for whenever you need us. You just have to ask. If it weren't for Mo here, collecting presents at Christmas and keeping an eye on you every morning, we'd have had no idea.'

'That's right,' added Mr Ghosh. 'He's always telling us how hard you work to help your mam. And you guys never ask for anything – even when you should. That prize is the least you deserve. We look after our own, we do, don't we, Mo? Proud of ya – you enjoy that, you hear?' And with a grunt and a wink, he disappeared behind the bush and back into his home.

As he left, Mam looked down at me and, touching my face with a shaking hand, whispered, 'I'm so proud of you, Audrey. More than you'll ever know.'

\*   \*   \*

At school that day, I showed the letter to Inara and Kavi and Mrs Li and Mr Garcia too. Soon everyone in school had heard I was going to meet Anthony Jones, the most famous Welsh actor ever, and that I was a Young Carer too. But now that I was an award-winning one, it didn't feel like something I had to hide any more. So I decided I wouldn't. Not ever again.

Over the next few days, Mam went through my little black book with me, and we did all the sums. It turned out that after I had paid everyone back, I'd only have thirty-nine pounds and sixty-seven pence left – which wasn't enough for even a wheel, let alone a whole wheelchair! I told Mam I wanted to buy the wheelchair first and that I could pay everyone back slowly with my stamp duty money, but Mam said absolutely not, and that being honest and having dignity was more important than material things. 'Besides,' she said, 'Dr Adeola is helping me with all the forms we need. So we shall hope for the best.'

But I didn't want to just hope for the best. Especially not if the people in power she spoke about weren't interested in our hopes. So I came up with a brand-new idea about how to help her get everything we needed – one that didn't involve a box or stamps, secret trains or getting into trouble with the police.

All that week and the weekend too, whenever Mam was OK and Kat and Peck were playing, I wrote out my very own letters, drew my very own stamps to go on them, and designed a poster too. I showed the posters to Inara and Kavi and Mrs Li before class register on Monday morning – the last Monday before Easter break.

'That is an excellent idea, Audrey,' said Mrs Li. 'And yes, of course I can photocopy the poster for you.'

'Yeah!' said Kavi. 'I'm in!'

'That's well wicked!' said Inara, rubbing her nose excitedly. 'Shall we start tonight? I'm free!'

We all agreed, so the second the bell for home-time rang Inara and Kavi and me ran to pick up Kat and Peck, and made our way to my street. One by one, we began knocking and ringing on the doors of all the neighbours on both sides of the house with the red door, and on both sides of my blue door too.

'I'm Audrey from number thirty-three,' I said to each of them. 'And this is my brother and sister Kat and Peck, and my best friends Inara and Kavi. And I wanted to say thank you for all the Christmas presents you bought for us – with Mo – and for being my evidence for the Light of Wales award too. This is for you.'

Kat or Peck handed them one of my extra-special thank-you letters, and Kavi or Inara handed over a poster.

'This is two posters in one,' I said, standing up straight like businesspeople did in the movies. 'The first side is for if you ever need your car washing. You can send a message through Mo to me, and we'll wash it for you right away. All the money will be going towards helping my mam get a wheelchair and a stairlift and a

273

bathroom – only please don't tell her that's what we're using the money for, because she doesn't know yet. It's a surprise. And the other side of the poster is to ask if you can help me give Mo an extra special thank-you street party this Sunday. Will you come?'

Everyone was so nice and nodded and smiled and said 'Definitely!' Mr Llewelyn said he'd bring some of his fold-out work-tables, and Mr Jahangir and his wife said they could bring us some snacks and chocolate, and Mrs Lumley said she'd make a big cake, and by the time we were done with all eleven houses, we had three cars to wash and a whole load of things for Mo and his thank-you street party.

'This is wicked!' said Inara as we made our way back to my house. 'We should get more of these printed out and go to all the streets in Abertawe! We can get your mam a brilliant wheelchair if we get more business. I'm going to ask my Aunt Husnara to help too! Maybe she can even do a massive fundraising drive at all her car washes. She's done it before for hospitals and refugees and things – she can raise loads of money for us!'

'That'd be awesome!' I cried out, instantly imagining

a huge line of sparkly cars with lots of people holding out lots of five-pound notes.

'Hey, we've got one poster and letter left,' said Kavi as we reached my gate. 'Have we missed someone?'

'Oh,' I said, frowning. In all the excitement, I had forgotten about the invisible spy at number forty-two. I stood and stared at the bright-red door, thinking hard. We hadn't heard anything from Sergeant Anita, and I hadn't seen any police people coming to knock on the door. It had been over a week now. What if there hadn't been anything to find? If it had been *Them*, wouldn't they have come and taken Mam or me away by now?

'I don't think anyone will answer the door,' I said. 'But give it to me anyway.'

Taking the poster from Kavi, I crossed the road and, walking right up to the red door, I rang the bell.

'Monster, come out!' whispered Kat, as she ran up and poked her fingers through the letterbox. Peck stood by Kavi and Inara as they all came and stood next to me.

I rang it again, and then a third time, but just as I'd expected, everything stayed sil—

275

'Yes?'

I stared up at the lady who had appeared in front of me with a sudden swish of the red door. She had a brown ponytail and was wearing a white cardi over the coolest dinosaur dungarees I had ever seen.

'Erm . . . I just – I just wanted to give this to . . .'

I held out the poster and quickly tried to take a look inside the house. But it was so dark I couldn't see a thing.

The woman smiled. 'Thank you – looks like an interesting poster. I'll pass this on to David. I'm sure he'd love you to wash his car again.'

'Again?' I asked. 'You mean – you – he – did see us then?'

The woman grinned at me. 'Yes – you're the girl who lives over the road, aren't you? Just across the street? You all washed his car and sent him a message in a turtle bottle, didn't you? That didn't half make him laugh. Thank you for that.'

'The spy's name is *David*?' blurted out Kavi.

'Spy?' asked the lady, frowning. 'He wishes!'

'But – the flashing lights – and the curtains – and no one opening the door and the—'

'The drone!' helped Inara.

For a few seconds the woman stared right back at all of us, but I could tell she was thinking because her eyeballs were moving from side to side. 'Flashing lights? Do you mean this?'

Taking what looked like a pen and a thermometer all rolled into one from the front pocket of her dungarees, she switched the end of it on and flashed a super-bright white light at us.

'That's it!' I cried out. 'That's exactly the light!'

'Ah. Well, that's just my thermo-pen,' explained the woman. 'David is very ill, you see. I'm his nurse, and sometimes I leave this here. I guess he must be using it to look for things or have a play with it when I'm not here. He does get awfully bored.'

'Does he have a drone?' asked Kavi, nervously chewing on what I was sure was five fruit pastilles all in one go. 'One that sounds like . . .' Kavi put his teeth together and made a strange squealing noise that sounded as if a small animal was stuck in a hole.

The woman's frown jumped up and then became deeper. 'Drone? What would we be doing with a drone?'

'But we heard a machine come up to the door,' I explained.

'The only machine we have here is David's wheelchair. It is quite a big one, so it is quite noisy.'

'Oh,' I said, thinking back to the noise and the thud. I realised the sound could have been an electric wheelchair approaching and bumping into the door.

'And – and there was that time when Mrs Lumley's dog was barking at the house because of all the drilling noises,' added Inara.

'Ah. We had a new stairlift fitted a few weeks ago. That was painful to listen to!'

'So how come David doesn't ever come outside? Or – or you?' I tried again. 'And how come you only come at night-time . . . and why has no one seen him?'

'And why's the house always dark, and why doesn't he use his car?' added Inara.

'GHOSTS!' shouted Peck, scaring himself.

The lady burst out laughing. 'You lot are a nosy bunch, aren't you? Well, let me put you out of your misery. We don't use the front door because the pavement out here has a huge kerb, see? Whereas the

278

pavement at the back has a ramp. So it's easier for him to use the back entrance.'

We all swung our heads round to check the pavement. I had never noticed before how high the kerb was. For someone in a wheelchair it wouldn't be easy to get up and down at all. I made a mental note to tell Mam about that for when she got her wheelchair.

'As for me, I park my car round the back too and let myself in that way because it's directly on my way home. Saves me from having to come up and down at least two hills to get to this side. And Mr Hall – David – has a very special skin condition, which means he has to stay away from all forms of direct sunlight. So that's why we have the curtains drawn during the day. I call him a vampire because he usually sleeps the day away and is up all night, and that's why he needs me to come check in on him at night-time. I only drop by during the daytime – like today – when he needs someone to sign for a timed parcel at the door. Or if he has someone like a plumber or someone due to come in and who probably won't find the back door. Today, I'm waiting on a new part for his wheelchair to be delivered . . . Should be here within the hour . . . It's all very lonely for him, but he copes rather well, I think. As for that car . . .'

The nurse carer leaned forward and, looking at the car, smiled. 'It used to belong to his wife. He can't ever drive again, sadly, but he keeps it to remember her by. He was so happy when you washed it.'

I took a step back and held my head in my hands as Kat and Peck happily whispered 'Vampires!' to each other. All this time I had thought the house on the other side of the street was hiding away a thief or a spy or an enemy who was going to destroy my world. When really it was just someone who sounded as brave as my mam and someone who deserved to be looked after too.

'Tell you what,' said the lady. 'Why don't I give David this lovely poster here, and maybe he'll be up for meeting you one day soon? He doesn't like people seeing him most of the time – he's very shy, but I think for you he might make an exception. That all right?'

I nodded happily as the woman said goodbye and began to shut the door.

'Sorry – but what's your name?' I asked quickly, before it had shut all the way.

The door reopened and, with a big smile that made her pink lipstick look like the outline of a crescent moon, the woman replied, 'Olivia,' before she shut the door all the way.

Inara and Kavi turned to stare at me, and I stared back at them, and then without knowing why, we all burst out into so much laughter that we nearly cried.

\* \* \*

The street party for Mo is just two days away now, and I can't wait. It's going to be the best party in the whole of Swansea! I'm using all the other stamps Mo gave me to make a banner that spells out a giant THANK YOU. And Kavi and Inara's mams and tads are going to be bringing lots of samosas and coconut pastries, and Mrs Davies is bringing crisps and sweets from her shop, and Mr Ghosh is going to be bringing flowers from his garden to decorate all of Mr Llewelyn's tables. Dr Adeola and Mrs Li are going to get drinks and cups, and Mr Garcia said he's going to ask his wife to bring her ice-cream van with her. I haven't told Inara because she'll probably die from happiness. And

Mam phoned the number Sergeant Anita had on her card and invited her too. I haven't told Kavi that, because then *he'd* die of happiness at the thought of meeting a police officer all the way from London, and then I'd be left with no best friends.

The best thing about the party is that it's not just Mo who'll be getting a surprise. Because while Mo doesn't know about the party, Mam has no idea what Mo, and my school, and Mrs Davies, and Inara's Aunt Husnara, have been doing since Inara had her brilliant idea about asking her aunt to help us. She doesn't know that for the last few days, Aunt Husnara has been asking *all* her customers at her car washes to donate to a new cause: my mam's wheelchair and stairlift! And that every day Mrs Li has been making lots of photocopies of the front side of my poster – except with a new bit telling people to 'GO TO A BUBBLES CAR WASH NEAR YOU AND HELP OUT OUR NEIGHBOUR!' Or that Mo has been posting the poster through all the letterboxes on all the streets he delivers letters to, and Mrs Davies has been giving it out to all her other Post Office friends to hang in their windows too.

I'm not sure how much Aunt Husnara has raised already, but Inara said she was going to come to the street party and make a special announcement, so I guess it'll be a surprise for me too.

I think it's the best thing ever, to go from feeling all alone with no one to turn to for help, to knowing there are lots of people looking out for you, even when you might not know it. It's just as exciting as seeing a brand-new stamp – except the roar is louder and lasts longer too. I'm lucky to have that feeling every day now, and I don't ever want it to end. I don't think it ever will. Not when I've got friends and neighbours like the ones I've got on my street in Swansea. And the best postman in the whole of the Milky Way, knocking on all our doors.

## Author's Note

When I was fifteen years old, as mock exams and GCSE finals and worries about picking the right college for A levels swamped my world, a life-altering catastrophe struck my household: my father injured his spine and became paralysed from the neck down, becoming fully immobile for over half a year.

In the midst of the trauma of seeing a healthy parent suddenly and literally floored, was the fact that I tried to hide the happenstance of my unexpectedly becoming a young carer from every single person I knew. For reasons I cannot yet fathom, I didn't want any of my friends – not even those I had grown up sharing my deepest fears and silliest crushes with, or any of my favourite teachers – knowing that I now had a paralysed father to care for when I got home. To have to admit that to anyone felt like an embarrassment I would never survive. Having spent years as a 'geek', a 'teacher's pet' and a 'four-eyes' trying to fit in at school, I had finally secured my own group of rather eccentric, albeit oft-bullied group of friends. Being singled out via another difference, and the prospect of endless pity, wasn't an option.

So all at once, my house – being situated three minutes from my school and often a safe haven for me and my friends – suddenly became a no-go zone. Gone were the mornings where friends would knock on my door so we could all walk to school together, or lunchtimes watching reruns of a comedy show. I told a million small lies to keep them from knocking on my door and finding out that my father was being cared for downstairs. Gone too were my after-school revision classes and basketball practice. With my mum now needing to work doubly hard to keep us all afloat and the bills paid, it was up to me to step up too, and look after my dad and my little brother whenever she was at work.

To this day, I rarely speak about this time of my life.

The fears, strains and tears that engulfed each day, coupled with my father's own frustrations at having to be cared for, forges a room whose door and windows I have locked and bolted, and never want to venture into ever again. And that's as someone who was incredibly lucky. Lucky enough to not become a carer until my teen years, as opposed to becoming one in my early years. Lucky enough not to have the worry of caring for someone without knowledge, training or experience for longer, because somehow, after nine months of strenuous therapy, my father miraculously managed to get back on his feet and become mobile and independent again.

If he hadn't, I'm not sure if I would be here, typing out these words for a fifth middle-grade book. If he hadn't, my life would most likely have gone a completely different way.

It is estimated that in the UK alone, there are over one million young carers. That in every single classroom there are at least two children – some as young as five years old – helping to care for a parent, a sibling, a grandparent, or some other person of their household when they get home. Many will never be identified as young carers – with Asian, South Asian and Black young carers being the most likely to go completely unnoticed, and therefore shut out from not only any form of recognition, but crucial support and respite.

How sad, how infuriating, that these children – these utter s/heroes of the universe, are looked over by so many governments, schools, platforms. How easy would it be to create a society where every young carer is supported, celebrated and encouraged to share their immense contributions to us all, with us all. And not be made to feel so alone.

Alongside the often hidden worlds in which young carers survive, there is another, oft-ignored group of people rarely recognised for the huge part they play in caring for people – for streets of people – in their own unique ways. That is, of course, the postal community.

As someone who grew up completely obsessed with stamps, people working for the Royal Mail and the Post Office were always figures of deep, immense magic to me. And why wouldn't they be, these oft-smiling, polite strangers, responsible for delivering envelopes of mystery?

But it wasn't until lockdown that I really understood

how important postmen and women are to so many. How they make up the eyes and ears of entire communities, many bravely approaching doors most of us will never have the chance to knock on. It is thanks to my own postman at the time, Abi, and my brother Zak (who worked as a postman for a summer), that the idea for this story took root. For it was through them that I learned of families looking for a bit of help with something, and heard often funny and beautiful tales of people doing incredible things for each other. I also grew aware that for too many souls, their postman/woman was the only face they would see and get to speak with each day.

With fewer and fewer children getting to experience the sheer joy of either sending or receiving a piece of mail in their name; and as the artistry and role of stamps in documenting historical moments, peoples and creations goes on being 'streamlined' for electronic versions, this story is, in hindsight, a letter of my own. One written for all the magnificent young carers of the world, keeping so many hearts beating in a million ways; for the amazing postmen and women crossing hundreds of thresholds each day to not only fulfil their duty, but to take on a duty of care that their job descriptions and pay do not stretch to; and lastly, for the creators and collectors, the senders and receivers of the 21mm by 24mm little squares whizzing around the planet right at this moment, linking us all in a million tiny life-changing ways . . .

# Acknowledgements

I was eight years old when an envelope dropped through the letterbox and immediately captured my attention and imagination. Bordered by red and blue diagonal lines, and penned with letters that flicked off at the side, it looked like a mini painting had landed on the corridor floor, centred by my mother's name. And in the corner, the master-stroke: a stamp showing a tiny man, with a pointy straw hat, wielding two buffaloes through a field of green so vibrant I could feel it.

The letter had travelled all the way from my grandparents in Bangladesh to our council flat in London's East End. It might as well have been sent from outer space so wondrous did this seem to me. What followed was a lifelong love of everything and anything to do with the magic of postal systems, and most especially stamps. A love always encouraged by Mum, who would return from her office some days with handfuls of stamps she had asked her colleagues to gather for me. From that day to this, hitting post offices wherever I travel in the world has become part and parcel of my adventures. So thank you Mum, and Nana and Nani, for imprinting upon me a deep appreciation for the beauty of letters and stamps alike. I hope this story does you proud.

This book would not have been birthed even as an idea if it hadn't been for Abi, my wonderful postman, who all throughout lockdown, when allowed to work, went out of his way to keep my whole street laughing and smiling, while keeping us abreast of who needed help where. What an honour to have a friend on my very doorstep, and to have met my very own Mo. Similarly, without the insight and hilarious stories of my beloved brother Zak, whose memories of working as a postman helped me solidify Mo in so many ways, this story would have remained a wispy figment. Thanks a million billion Zak (and, er . . . I'm sorry I ever wished you'd disappear overnight when we were kids so I could finally have a sister. Am glad God didn't listen).

To Silvia Molteni, who continues to be my special-delivery mailwoman, thank you for always knocking on doors for me, and for ensuring the stories I want to tell don't get lost in the many conveyor belts of the world. I am so thankful, every day, for your guidance and wisdom, and for having my back whatever the challenges. No matter how late or delayed my works, your faith that I can deliver something worthwhile keeps me going. Thank you.

Lena McCauley: we did it! And here it goes, out into the letterboxes of the world so to speak. Thank you for your patience, and for understanding exactly where this story needed to go, and why. I hope you're as proud of this story as I am, and that one day, your very own special package will grow up to appreciate the part you have played in all my stories. Both they – and Audrey Hepburn! – have a lot to thank you for!

Forging the final cover of this book was as painful as I imagine stamp duty to be, but you did it, Pippa Curnick! You gifted the cover of Audrey's dreams, and I am deeply and eternally grateful for it. This story could never have gone out into the world with anything else. I hope it makes you smile whenever you spot it out in the world . . .

Nazima Abdillahi, Laura Pritchard, Alison Padley and all the editorial and marketing teams at Hachette: thank you for lending this story your eagle eyes and expertise. I am grateful that the army it takes to get a story out in the world is led by you all. And Dominic Kingston: thank you, as always, for keeping forty gazillion plates (I counted!) spinning in my book worlds, despite all attempts to throw them off course by so many.

My heartfelt thanks to: Matthew Harris of the Royal Mail Group for your swift and kind responses; the wonderful teams at the Postal Museum for bearing with my million questions and requests to ride the Mail Rail at least thirteen times!; the magnificent-of-heart Sharandeep Sahota, national Changemakers Award winner and wondrous carer of her beautiful grandparents, for teaching me so much about 'seva' – selfless service – in such a short amount of time (you are deeply wonderful and have inspired me so much); the tireless wonder that is Blake Leonard, creator of Chocs for

Champs, for being an emblem of kindness and caring to so many children and adults alike; Holly Swinckels of Carers Trust UK for your swift and deeply kind responses to our queries; Andy McGowan of Caring Together Cambridgeshire and Janice Styles of Carers in Bedfordshire for your generosity of hearts and all the works you both do for our s/heroes (thank you, Jude Habib, for the wonderful introductions!); and all the young carers I have had the honour of meeting through both Making Herstory and O's Refugee Aid Team, who go out of their ways to help their mothers especially survive experiences no-one should have to bear. Every single one of you put so many of this world to shame by your forbearance and dignity in the face of so many obstacles placed before you. Keep going.

To my nephews and nieces in Swansea, Wales: I love that our times together have led to a story being forged in our mutual dragon's heartland. Kamilah and Inara: this one's for both of you especially . . . Race you to Bracelet Bay for a hot chocolate and a read!

To my universe of staggeringly beautiful and wise friends (whose names I would need a few more pages to list), thank you for keeping me going in a million and one ways – and for never letting me lose the faith. You know who you are, and just how much I love you. Susan Wilkins: how gorgeous to have you as a new addition to my works and family. Thank you for lightening a thousand loads in one fell swoop – all whilst singing Taylor Swift at me (yeahy!).

And last but never least, my eternal letters of gratitude continue to be mailed out to God each and every second of each and every day. May they be delivered swiftly and surely, and never go astray.

# What is a Young Carer?

A young carer is a very special person between 5 to 18 years old, who helps to look after someone in need of daily assistance. The person needing their help might be their mum or dad, a grandparent, a brother or sister, other relatives like an uncle or aunt, or a family friend or neighbour.

In this story, Audrey is a young carer because she takes care of her mum – and her brother and sister too.

# Are YOU a Young Carer?

Young carers might have to help the person they are caring for by:

- Helping them get out of / into bed
- Helping them change clothes
- Doing the cleaning and washing
- Making meals on a regular basis
- Doing the shopping
- Helping to manage money / bills
- Getting / giving medication
- Accompanying them to doctors' appointments
- Listening and calming them down when they get upset
- Helping to look after other people so they don't have to worry

Sometimes, because of all their caring duties, young carers miss out on going to school, or aren't able to do things that everyone else their age gets to do (like going to sports practice, or joining an after-school club).

It also means they might be worried and stressed about the person they care for on a regular basis.

## Did You Know?

There are at least one MILLION young carers in the United Kingdom alone.

It is estimated that at least TWO CHILDREN in every classroom is a young carer. That includes children as young as 5 years old.

Real figures could be much, much higher.

But sadly, lots of young carers never tell anyone they are caring for people, so the real figures remain unknown.

# If You Are a Young Carer...

First of all, Thank You for being an awesome human being. Second of all, did you know you can get help and support for yourself and all your family by registering as a Young Carer?

Lots of children *don't* do this, which means they miss out on lots of exciting opportunities and aid and the chance to make friends with other carers in their local area. There are lots of charities that host Young Carers festivals and special programmes to help you take a break from your caring duties.

Ask a parent/guardian to help you find your nearest Young Carers support branch so that you can get help for yourself and everyone you love. You can do this by going to:

**Carers Trust UK** at: **www.carers.org** and typing in your postcode. OR you can call the **Carers Direct helpline** on **0300 123 1053**. If you are deaf, deafblind, hard of hearing or have impaired speech, you can also contact the **Carers Direct helpline** using textphone or minicom number 0300 123 1004.

## If You Are a Parent / Guardian of a Young Carer...

If you are the parent/guardian of a young carer, or a carer too, and would like to speak with someone in confidence about any worries or stresses you are feeling, please contact: **Family Lives** at **www.familylives.org.uk** (live chat options) Or call the free helpline on **0808 800 2222**.

## If You Are a Teacher / Professional ...

For teachers and professionals working with young carers who would like to access resources and training to ensure young carers are identified and aided in your worlds, please contact: **Children's Society** at **www. childrenssociety.org.uk**

## Five Fun Facts About Stamps...

1. The special name given to someone who likes to collect or study stamps (just like Audrey does) is a philatelist.

2. The first ever non-royal person to appear on a UK stamp was William Shakespeare. Before he appeared on stamps in 1964, only members of the Royal Family were allowed to appear on stamps!

3. The most expensive – and rarest – stamp in the whole wide world, is the British Guiana 1c Magenta: a red octagon-shaped stamp that is the only one of its kind known to exist. Created in 1856 as an emergency stamp, it was found in 1873 by a little boy – who sold it for just six shillings. Today, it is worth over £9MILLION!

4. There are not many things that increase in price if something goes wrong. But not so with stamps!

5. If an error occurs in the production of a stamp sheet – such as designs being printed upside down, or colours coming out wrong, or errors in the holes (perforations) along the borders – the stamps

instantly become unique. Which means they can sell for thousands and even millions of pounds! (So, if you see a stamp that doesn't look quite right, keep hold of it!)

## Did You Know?

The oldest philatelic society in the whole world is based in . . . the UK! Established in 1869, the Royal Philatelic Society London has a HUGE library and collection of old stamps and designs. Anyone with a love of stamps can join on application and become a member upon approval. There is even an Associate Membership offering for young philatelists aged 14 upwards. If you are interested in joining and learning more about the society, see **www.rpsl.org.uk**. (Hmmm . . . I wonder if Mo is already a member . . .)

## The Real Mail Rail ...

Yup! The mail rail in this book that Audrey jumps on to is based on a real-life underground train, specially built to carry just post (not people)!

Today, the mail rail is looked after by the Postal Museum in London and allows visitors to take a ride on it (making it, quite possibly, the best museum on the planet)!

Here are a four amazing facts about one of the most famous secret little trains in the world . . .

1. In February 1928, the Mail Rail became the first ever electric railway system to work without drivers!

2. When the Mail Rail was at its busiest, it carried more than six million bags of mail every year. That equates to over 4 million letters every single day! The effort to make sure everything got delivered on time took over 200 postal workers to ensure the trains – and London's post – kept moving 22 hours a day.

3. During the First World War, the Rail Mail tunnels were used to hide treasures from the British

Museum, the Tate and the National Portrait Gallery
– including the Rosetta Stone – to protect them all
from the bombs.

4. The Mail Rail carried letters and parcels across
London from 1927 until it was shut down in 2003.
Now it carries people who love post (including
Audrey).

Learn more about the Mail Rail and take a wander
through time, stamps and history at the **Postal Museum**
at **www.postalmuseum.org**.

Who knows, you might meet a postman called Mo
there . . .

## The Stamp Challenge!

Here are three challenges Audrey and Mo would like to set you! See if you can fulfil them all . . .

1.  **Start a competition in your class or in your family** to see who can collect the most stamps in one month. Then hold a special vote for the best, most interesting stamp collected!

**Did You Know?** Stamps from around the world often have beautiful pictures, symbols and colours linked to special things in their country.

2.  **Design a stamp that represents your school/town/ city.** Are there any animals, colours, people or local heroes you would include in your stamp? What or who would they be, and why?

**Did You Know?** Every year, the Royal Mail releases Special Stamp Issues – special edition stamp collection packets, celebrating everything from books, authors, films, characters and famous people, to cars, flowers, constellations and animals.

3. **Pick your favourite book to create a Special Stamp Issue about.** Pick four of your best-loved, most favourite moments from that book and turn them into four individual stamp drawings.

If you really, really, REALLY love the book, pick eight scenes (as Special Stamp Issues usually come in 'books' of eight stamps), and draw out all eight of those scenes.

For inspiration, take a look at the **Royal Mail website at www.royalmail.com.**

# Onjali Q. Raúf

Photo © Rehan Malik

Onjali Q. Raúf is the founder of Making Herstory, an organisation that encourages men, women and children to work together to create a fairer and more equal world for women and girls everywhere; and O's Refugee Aid Team through which she delivers emergency aid and support for frontline refugee aid response teams in northern France and Greece. She was awarded an MBE in 2022 for her services to literature and women's rights.

She is the author of *The Boy at the Back of the Class*, *The Star Outside My Window*, *The Day We Met The Queen*, *The Night Bus Hero*, *The Lion Above the Door*, *Hope on the Horizon* and *Where Magic Grows*.